Anything He Wants

stories

Richard Weems

WbW Ink   New Jersey

ISBN: 0-9974332-1-3
ISBN-13: 978-0-9974332-1-0

WbW Ink
28 Rockridge Rd.
Haskell, NJ 07420

www.facebook.com/CheapStories

For Svea, my BabyMine

Also by Richard Weems:

The Cheap Stories eBook series

The Way of It: New and Selected Cheap Stories

Stark Raving Blue

From Now On, You're Back

CONTENTS

ACKNOWLEDGMENTS

Thanks to the following publications for first publishing previous versions of these stories:

The Beloit Fiction Journal - "Leaving"
Gettysburg Review - "Anything He Wants"
Florida Review - "The Hunt"
Other Voices - "Artistic Endeavor"
Inscape Magazine - "The Cat Story"
Night Train - "Dogs"
Morpo Review - "The Woman and the Dog"
The Mississippi Review - "Mrs. Boylan, Widowed"
jerseyworks - "The Taffy Pull"
Gulf Stream Magazine - "Homecoming"

NOTE: This is an expanded edition of the original publication of *Anything He Wants*, with an additional story.

LEAVING

Katie the real estate agent calls ahead when there are more prospective buyers to show the house to, and when Katie calls, my wife Rhonda goes to work. She wipes down the living and dining room walls with wet rags, puts the dishes away, takes the laundry down from the backyard clothesline, vacuums. Sometimes I hear her stir up a pitcher of lemonade. From lemons, not a mix. I can hear all this from my bed because the walls still need insulation. They're cellophane-thin with respect to noise; I can hear things even in the basement. Because of this, I'm not supposed to sleep when Katie's showing the house off. I snore, quite loudly when too much fluid has built up in my lungs. Since I have to stay awake, there's little else for me to do but eavesdrop. Katie and Rhonda show prospective buyers the upstairs, but they make it a point not to show anyone my room; Katie is sure the sight of a dying man in bed won't help sell the place.

Katie is quite good at this business. As she passes by my room, in the middle of rattling off the dimensions to the upstairs, and what work needs to be done, and where, she'll say towards my door, "This room we can't look in on right now," probably with a womanly wave of the back of her hand, and that's usually the end of it. Few people pry, and those who do aren't given an answer and soon stop asking for one. Katie is an easy six feet in height, brunette (an imposing figure), and she knows how to sell a house. She doesn't tie her hair back. I've only met her face-to-face once, when Rhonda brought her in to see me and introduced her as the woman who is going to get our house sold. She carries a clipboard. I honestly don't think she uses it, but carries it to make herself look even more businesslike.

The house itself is a steal. Rhonda wants to sell it off quickly because it's killing me, and there won't be enough money to get away with until either the house is sold or I die and the insurance comes through. I wanted to give whoever bought the house the same deal I got—low price, many repairs needed—and I wanted him to have it better than I ever did. After my collapse, I had Rhonda make a list of all the needed repair-work I could remember and give it to Katie, and I wanted to throw in all my tools and hardware that are sitting in my shed in the backyard. I never got as far as using the portable jigsaw or the Black and Decker sander, and though I didn't take care of what I did use (a few of the brushes are so crusted with paint you could probably drive nails with them), I have four cans of turpentine out there, and WD-40, and a dip that should take care of the rusted hammers and other hand tools. There were days when I worked myself so tired that taking the tools back outside and cleaning them was too much to even consider, my joints would ache so badly (the cancer's spread even to them, I'm sure of it). A little cleaning and a little grease, and the power tools will work like new again. There's a rack of drill bits out there, half-inch to a sixty-fourth: more than I ever got around to using.

While showing the prospective buyers around, Katie recites my list of necessary repairs. After a little more than two months at roughly five tours a week, she has the whole list memorized. In the dining room, she points out the cracks in the ceiling and the stain line from the leaky water pipe behind the wall, and while going up the stairs she mentions how the banister needs to be reinforced and how some of the railing balusters are loose and how the treads of the top three steps need to be replaced. Once, Katie even kicked out one of the balusters to make her point.

I have needed to change that list occasionally. Being confined to bed, I've had much time to think, and getting that list just right was more important than getting better. I thought that getting this house fixed up, even if Rhonda and I weren't here to see it happen, would forgive me for my failures at both this house and our marriage. The downstairs bathroom, for example, didn't just need some new pipes (I suggested copper), but a whole new toilet. I once took a look at the date on the American Standard in there and was surprised: it was only thirty years old, nearly half my age. Thirty years, and already the house is falling apart. Whenever I thought of any new or revised repairs, I would tell them to Rhonda when she brought me my evening bowl of soup, a staple of the sick. Though Rhonda would frown and put out her lower lip and look worried when I told her these things, she usually got the message to Katie, but when she didn't, it was all I could do to keep from yelling out when I heard Katie rattle off the old items. Once, I didn't contain myself and shouted out that the frame of the far left bay window in the dining room needed to be refitted. I heard Katie stop halfway into a sentence, and soon enough, Rhonda came up to tell me not to excite myself. I felt sorry for bursting out like that because I realized I must have sounded like the ghost of a home-repair nut in the walls. I must have spooked those prospective buyers badly, because they've never come back. I didn't want to scare anyone off, but I didn't want any false impressions about this house. I used to think that I'd actually like it if Katie told buyers that I had collapsed of exhaustion while trying to plaster the holes in the guest-room ceiling.

A few people have come back to look the house over again. These are the only prospective buyers I ever get to see, since only returning buyers are shown the backyard and the outlying property. When Katie goes outside with these people, I get to my knees in bed and take a peek out the window over the varnished oak headboard. I look these people over and decide if I like them, if they look like people who are willing to do the work this house needs. Katie's hair shines in the sunlight. She usually wears a light-brown suit jacket with a plaid skirt, and though it looks hot on her, she doesn't seem to mind. I have to get up in bed carefully, so as to not make any of the floorboards creak and cause Rhonda any worry. She frets over me so much now that she blames herself when I black out or don't digest one of her soups well. If she ever caught me looking out into the backyard (though it's doubtful, since I can hear her coming all the way from the creaky bottom step of the staircase), she would scold herself for leaving me alone with nothing to do when buyers come and from then on let Katie show off the house by herself. Rhonda would have left me by now if I hadn't fallen sick. It's what makes my dying a convenience. Her settlement will be much easier to determine.

There's one guy I liked from the beginning who has come back four times already. Katie introduced him to Rhonda as Bruce DeSanders, Bruce DeSanders and his wife. He stays inside most of the time and concentrates on the house itself, so I've only seen him once, and that was a glimpse from behind. He stepped out into the backyard to talk to his wife, Sharon. Sharon I've seen much more of. She seems more interested in the grounds; she's gone straight into the backyard each time she and her husband have come back, and she stays out there until Bruce is ready to leave. The last couple of times, I've gotten to my knees as soon as I've heard Rhonda greet Mr. DeSanders, and within seconds Sharon has come out into the back.

The house is on ten acres. The five acres behind the house are jointly owned with the guy in the next lot, a man I've never met. From my window, the floodlight on his back porch is only a little larger than a pinpoint of light with a slight aura through the trees, except when there's a storm and the branches are being blown about, and then all I can see is a faint glow. There's a solid stretch of trees from my house to his. It's why I have the chainsaw, a good, long one that could easily cut down the young oaks nearest the house. The elms wouldn't be much of a problem, either. A fence could be put up. The one thick oak that's too thick to cut could be used for shade, and a tire could be strung from the lowest bough. I have a used Goodyear in the garage that would be perfect. It's a clean and sturdy whitewall with most of the tread worn down. I wanted the DeSanderses to have all my plans.

All I've ever seen Sharon wear are sun dresses—one is lime green, one sky blue, one a peach-like orange (she's worn this one twice)—and a broad-rimmed white straw hat, the kind old women wear to the beach, though Sharon is not old. Mid-late twenties is my guess, and by the look of her husband's back, Bruce is about the same age (though I'm under the impression that Sharon is the older of the two). While her husband inspects the state of the house, Sharon wanders around the backyard dreamily. Shading her eyes from the sun, she leans against the thick oak and looks up into its branches. She has curly brown hair and I have yet to see her smile. I've seen her put her hands to her stomach and press herself gingerly. I think she's pregnant. Rhonda has gone out to talk to her a few times and offer lemonade, but the two never talk long, as if they have nothing to say. They almost look related, standing next to each other.

I have gardening tools in my shed too. I have a crate of seed packets (radishes, lettuce, eggplant, all that), sacks of fertilizer, plant shovels, and a Garden Weasel. I have tomato stakes. Rhonda bought me these things when the cancer started hitting me bad and I was having problems with the house and such. She first bought me these things as something to mock me with, as more tools she thought I wouldn't be able to use. She even told me, as she presented me with these items, she had every confidence that I might at least be able to raise some radishes if I worked hard enough at it. I cursed her and threw her gardening idea ("Crap," I called it) and the tools into a pile in that corner of my shed and vowed to her and all the surrounding trees never to touch them. Later, I calmed down and stacked these things neatly, though I was sure I was never going to use them. After my collapse, she moved her things from the small bedroom down the hall back in with me. She carries her guilt quietly, and there are times when she thinks I am asleep when I've seen her looking at me and frowning to herself, but she's never felt bad enough to apologize. I once saw Sharon reach down and take a handful of dirt in the backyard. She's no stranger to tilling soil. She sifted the dirt in her hand, studied it, poked at it.

What struck me about this Bruce DeSanders was that he seemed to know his stuff. I heard him tell Katie how much flooding this house gets in the spring, and he figured this out from the watermark on the basement walls. He figured out the age of the house from the style of the bathroom fixtures alone: according to him, these faucets have not been made in twenty-five years. I made him out to be either someone looking to fix the house up and then sell it for a profit, or someone who's fixed up other people's houses for a living and now wants to do one for himself. The one time I saw him in the light, he was wearing a white T-shirt and jeans. His back was broad and strong: a worker. He had a full head of brown hair that came down below his shoulders. He came out to the edge of my view from the window and called to his wife. I couldn't make out what he said to her, but Sharon agreed to it, and Bruce went back into the house. Sharon still looks pleased with her husband, though I doubt they are newlyweds. Bruce DeSanders's footsteps are heavy, as if he wears boots.

After prospective buyers and Katie leave, Rhonda usually comes upstairs to check on me and tell me what she thinks. I've asked if she likes the DeSanderses, and she thinks they're nice, but she's never had as much hope for them as I did. Rhonda sits on the edge of the bed, tracing the butterfly patterns on my comforter with her finger, telling me about whoever came by that day, and she even absent-mindedly tucks in the corners of the comforter. I'm usually quite tired from keeping myself awake so long and am ready to sleep anyway. Sometimes I take Rhonda's hand as I fall asleep and I squeeze it for as long as I can because I'm not sure if I'm going to be alive long enough to wake up again. I usually sleep through to dinner, when Rhonda wakes me so I can take my medicine and eat, and then I'll sleep until the wee hours, waking with Rhonda beside me, though not curled up against my side as we used to sleep. Her guilt is sweet and pathetic, as if our gardening fight had something to do with my condition. I've been coming to realize maybe I yelled at her because there was no one else to yell at. I haven't told her this yet. I'm keeping it for my dying words.

I bought the house wanting a home, rebuilt with my own hands, that would shine from a distance, and I would wear a blue fishing cap with no hooks in it and enjoy my retirement and get some sun in the backyard in the summertime. I moved me and Rhonda from a small but comfortable one-story house in Manahawkin to this Chestnut Hill monstrosity that has tapped all my money: three floors, including the full attic, ten rooms, three bathrooms (one downstairs, two up), and something wrong everywhere. For thirty years I taught high-school juniors how to build miniature houses with working light-fixtures and insulation in the walls and shingles on the roofs and I thought I could do this for myself. Sometimes, when the kids were having trouble, I hinged the scaled-down doors or sanded the miniature frame of two-by-fours myself, and I was good at it. I put the best houses, the ones with working shutters and flush nails, on display in the shop room, for the freshmen and sophomores to admire when they came in to make their paperweights and monogrammed pencil holders.

When Rhonda and I first moved here in August, figuring three months would give me enough time to at least replace the windows, get the heater repaired, and insulate before the cold weather came, we spent a lot of time outside. Rhonda lounged in a green, collapsible beach-chair in the shade of the thick oak, and I walked around and around her, neither of us yet knowing how cancerous I really was. I read from my blueprints and described to Rhonda all my plans for the house. I could see the entire outside done over in an even shade of light gray that looks white from a distance but doesn't show dirt off so easily, and I could see blue shutters on all the windows. I saw the small trees cleared away, stumps and all, and a tall redwood fence with three gates. I saw a six-inch-thick layer of elm-tree mulch bordering the fence and plants sprouting from it. Rhonda lounged quietly, no umbrella, reading *Reader's Digest*, nodding and saying, "Yes, Roger," whenever I needed to hear it. Some days she wore her bright blue one-piece bathing suit that reflected all light, it seemed. She beamed: you had to shade your eyes to look at her.

I know I must be getting pale from having been inside for so long. Fortunately, Rhonda lets me keep the blinds open, but the curtains drawn. The curtains are white and as thin as veils almost. They glow when the sun is on this side of the house, coming in here only slightly dimmed and with shadows of lace, plus I managed to paint the wall facing the bed white before I stopped working, so the room is kept rather bright. It's too bright, I think now. I know I'm fading away.

It was March when I collapsed, the air still cold. I don't know how Rhonda and I made it through that winter, with the numbing cold and us sleeping separate so often, though there were nights when we put away our anger to keep each other from freezing. Rhonda was threatening to move to a motel where there was some heat. I was plastering holes in the guest room and wearing a flannel shirt and vest and I was wearing thermal underwear underneath it all. Rhonda warned me if I sweated too hard I would get my clothes damp and then catch cold on top of everything. Though my coughing fits weren't as frequent as usual, when they did hit I had to stop for five minutes at a time until I coughed up some fluid, which wasn't easy to do up on a stepladder and holding a mortarboard of plaster. I was so tired, I could barely see. I had to focus on my image of the house finished to keep me going.

I had a coughing fit so hard I got lightheaded and fell off the ladder. I landed on my stomach, my face hitting the floor hard, but I hardly felt it. I heard Rhonda rush out of the kitchen and start upstairs, probably fearing the worst, but I remember most distinctly how cool the floorboards felt against my cheek and temple. I didn't know a bare floor could get so cool. It was nice to feel so cool. I wished Rhonda hadn't heard me fall. I wanted to feel the floor, the cracks between the boards pressing into my cheek, for a little while longer before I died.

I was told to keep to bed, but I fought the doctors at first. I was out of control, obsessed with a house. Whenever Rhonda left me alone, I got up and went to work in the bedroom, oiling the hinges to the bedroom door or replacing the washer in the bathroom faucet. I remember that it actually hurt me, deep in the stomach, a nervous tightening, when I'd look at the house unfinished. It was like a kick in the stomach. I thought that, if I could just get the house together, everything would be right. Rhonda was sleeping with me again, but she didn't love me, and I thought being able to offer her a house was the least I could do.

Also, I wanted this house finished. I wanted to show Rhonda and anyone else who cared to know that I could do it. Once, I even got up on a stepladder and tried replacing the light fixture in the walk-in closet. The replacement had been sitting on the bureau, and the sight of it was annoying me more every day, but I lost my balance while removing the old fixture and almost had another fall. I've pretty much settled down, especially since last Wednesday night, but Rhonda still doesn't trust me: she moved all my tools out into the shed and makes it a point to check on me periodically. She's been working in the backyard lately, clearing weeds. Stray dogs and neglect have played havoc there, but Rhonda has opened up a couple of spots, dark with rich topsoil, even though we both know the house is going to be sold off soon. I'm sure she knows I get up to watch her work, but she won't admit it.

Late last Wednesday night, Rhonda was asleep. I was wide awake since no prospective buyers had come by. I had slept all day, and I heard somebody walking slowly through the dry ivy that I had pulled down from the side of the house, the pile I have on the list to burn. The footsteps were careful, but

9

still noisy enough for me to hear. I didn't have a gun, but I got out of bed slowly and went to the window at the end of the hall that opened over the ivy pile. I have no idea what I would have done if there had been a burglar out there, but I had to go to the window just the same. It was still my house.

The footsteps stopped as I forced the window open (it was a warped frame). The house is a hundred yards off the main road, so the only light was the neighbor's pinpoint past the trees. I could hear the breeze rustle leaves and the uncut grass.

I leaned out and said, "Who's there?" I knew exactly where the ivy pile was, but all I could see was the faint blur of a white shirt in the darkness. There was no response, and when I saw that hint of white start to move again, slowly, I called out again, and only then did the figure respond, "I've been here before." I recognized his voice immediately, though he sounded nervous. His voice shook a little, and I realized he had no idea who I was, or what I might be holding.

"I've been here a few times before," Bruce DeSanders said, his voice still shaking slightly. "I was thinking of buying the house. I just wanted to see how well-lit the property was at night." He paused a moment, then he said, "I'm sorry." With my eyes adjusting to the dark, his white shirt looked like a porcelain vase with large handles floating over the side yard. I couldn't make out anything else, it was so dark.

"Mr. DeSanders," I called, and he must have been quite surprised that I knew him so readily. "Mr. DeSanders, you could check this another time, couldn't you? It's quite late."

"Yes, of course," Bruce DeSanders said. "I'm sorry I woke you."

"I wasn't asleep," I said. Bruce DeSanders still sounded uncomfortable, so I clapped my hands together, as if I were wiping something from them, to show that they were empty.

"Well, I'm sorry just the same," he said.

For a moment I wanted to ask Bruce DeSanders if his wife Sharon liked the place, if she was out there somewhere, maybe waiting for him in his car, how much experience he had at house repair, what he intended to do with my house, but I had to cough again, and when the fluid finally came up it dribbled out. I heard it land like a large raindrop in the ivy. The coughing made me dizzy, and I leaned against the sill with my head down. I felt ashamed. The house wasn't mine. It had been Bruce DeSanders's house ever since he first looked it over. He knew what was wrong with it without Katie having to tell him a thing. Sharon was pregnant, he was young and strong and he knew how to fix a house, a true-to-life house, full-size, not something high-schoolers made, and I knew then that he was going to do this house up right. While trying to get my strength back, I heard Bruce DeSanders say quietly, "I'm terribly sorry," and he hurried away toward the road, where soon I heard a truck start.

I went to bed and lay there, looking up at the ceiling. I still was not sleepy. I remembered the stars at my old one-story house in Manahawkin. The previous owner had stuck glow-in-the-dark stars to the bedroom ceiling. When Rhonda and I first moved in, the stars no longer glowed except when the day had been particularly bright, and then only for a half hour or so just after nightfall. Whoever had done the sticking-up had no concept of constellations, but when those stars did glow, the ceiling looked vast. For a moment, I wanted those stars there, up on the ceiling above me. Rhonda moaned in her sleep as she does every now and then, but she kept to her side of the bed.

The DeSanderses are returning. What frightens me the most is that Bruce DeSanders is probably going to want to see my bedroom. To be sure no one sneaks in, Rhonda locks the door, and Katie is quite insistent about no one being shown in, but none of this is going to stop him. He's going to burst in and find me here, pale, withered and tired, and immersed in light. He's not going to look anything like me, and it's a scary thought. He's going to look at me and know I was the one who had done all this shoddy work he's been looking over each time he has come. He's going to put this house to rights without my help at all.

ANYTHING HE WANTS

Hamilton managed to show up on my front stoop again, his hair nappy and wild, dirt crusting up his beard.

"I've seen diarrhea look tastier," I said.

"Shut up, fuck-o," he said in greeting. "Had to hole up on a construction site last night." His pants were rumpled, the tattered coat obviously not his. "I couldn't remember your address. A rent-a-cop put his flashlight on me, so I dropped a brick on him and slept at a bus stop."

When I served my first and third turns for possession with intent, I managed my way into Hamilton's select crew. This kept a lot of bad characters off me, but it also put a permanent IOU in Hamilton's pocket. He'd used my apartment once before in the year and a half since my release. We stayed high for two days straight and he burned a hole in the carpet. Before he left he made me give him two hundred dollars and all my loose change. I would have preferred never opening my door to Hamilton again, but turn away a guy like him, with a good number of assaults on his rap sheet among other things, and you only give him reason to come back sooner, the next time with a grudge. If he hadn't spotted me peeking through my bedroom curtains, I would have pretended I wasn't home.

Hamilton took a step forward, and I made room. Hamilton didn't care if you wanted a guest or not. His coat was thick with a smoky street smell. I followed him to the living room and took a seat in the middle of the sofa while he patted his pockets and moved about as though he had lost something. I put my head back, despite the danger of nodding out. I worked the overnight shift, and Hamilton had brought me out of my first good sleep in days. Hamilton looked over the walls as though seeing the apartment for the first time, as if looking to buy.

"Who do you have to report to?" I figured some talk would keep me awake.

"They gave me a card," Hamilton said. He settled into the plush chair and studied the upholstery on the armrest. He brushed it against the grain and smoothed it down again. "Won't be seeing much of him. These guys have nothing new to tell me."

"The bastard should thank you for that," I said.

"Got a ride to town from a couple on their way to the Kiss Farewell Tour." Hamilton started ripping up fuzz and threads of fabric from the armrest. "Figured they'd give a poor slob a lift, do their deed for the day. 'Farewell Tour-my-ass,' I told them." He turned and pointed at me to emphasize this last statement, then he went back to his business with the armrest. "Kids going to see a bunch of old men wearing makeup for the paycheck, and they didn't have any shit on them, not even a bottle. She was nice. I could've taken them off the road and made him watch as I worked her over." Hamilton cracked his neck.

I had a girlfriend now, Deborah, who I'd met three months ago at the NA group I didn't go to anymore. She worked days, waiting tables at a diner called The Circle, so for the moment there was no chance of her barging in and Hamilton getting the kinds of thoughts he got. But she did live in the apartment upstairs. I stared at the drop ceiling as though connecting some of those holes would offer up a solution.

"We need movies," Hamilton said. "Something fucking Stephen Segal. Something kung fu. Nothing but fem-flicks Friday nights last month. The kind of shit you toss lit cigarettes at."

"Oprah Book Club category?" I asked. My forehead was getting tight. I rubbed it and squeezed my eyes shut. In that darkness, I could see a damn painful headache approaching like dense fog.

"More like Sally Struthers." Hamilton laughed at what he was about to say. "All sensitive and bovine."

"They got a channel now," I said. "Sappy movies like that all day."

I had to think of a way to get a message to Deborah. She wasn't going to understand, but I knew it was best we pretend not to know each other for a while. Most people would have doubts when an addict and convicted dealer says he wants to stay out for good this time, but Deborah was holding me to my word. She was keeping me away from the bars and parking lots where I'd done business. I still bought smack once a month from a Latino toilet-scrubber at the office building I cleaned, but to Deborah what mattered most was that I was working myself off it. When I complained about how empty and lonely the road to the straight and narrow looked, she got a geometry teacher who was a regular at The Circle to go out fishing with me. I hadn't been fishing in ten years, since high school. We dragged for fluke off Barnegat Light. I still remembered the old trick of using minnow and squid on the same hook.

The headache had its claws in me now, making base camp somewhere behind my nose. I needed smack or sleep, something to numb me out so the pain could run its course, but I didn't want to show Hamilton my stash. You didn't show Hamilton anything you didn't want him taking away. He had already worked through the upholstery of the armrest and was pulling out the stuffing in thick, cobwebby strands.

Hamilton looked like any inmate fresh from the hole: homeless, aimless, bored already with the outside, looking to grab anything that made the free world real. "We need a bucket of wings," he said. "Chips and salsa. I haven't seen a bowl full of chips in too long. I could eat those things all day." He found something of interest about a strand he'd just pulled up. "I could fuck a wall right now," he said. "I could fuck a chimp."

"There, I can't help you," I said. Deborah kept tabs on me with a lonely, needy kind of insistence, and when she started acting too much like we were married, I'd tell her she looked chunky in her uniform or that her pancakes tasted like chalk. Still, when I refused to let her move in here, she moved in upstairs. This was reason alone to protect her, and the longer Hamilton was thinking of staying, the better the chances they'd be running into each other.

The headache had swelled into a grape, leaden and hollow. I had that feeling of things going bad for a while. Hamilton had no intention of leaving any time soon. Shit, he had no intention of doing anything but what damn well pleased him, and right now he was squeezing himself through his pants.

When we first met, Hamilton was on his fourth time through: car theft, possession of an unlicensed .22 and he threw a full bottle of Crazy Horse at the arresting officer. By the time I started my third turn, he was back in for bashing a guy's skull on a bar rail. When the heat came down, he was tearing the sweater off the wounded man's girlfriend. All this because Hamilton thought the guy had laughed at him. Hamilton could have gotten up and put the plush chair through the window and given me no better reason than it was comfortable and matched the sofa. Maybe Hamilton wasn't planning to make his way back to jail again, but some assholes just can't help themselves.

"You got to take a ride to Atlantic City if you're looking to score ass," I said. I would have paid the bus fare and given him pocket money if it had come to that.

"Fuck," Hamilton said. He leaned back and put his hand on the side of his face. "You holding?"

It was safe to hide things from Hamilton as long as he never found out, but flat-out lying was hazardous road conditions. I was too tired to get my stash for him, so I directed him to the kitchen. He got the baggie from the utensil drawer and my bottle of Gordon's too. While he cooked up a shot and pulled from the gin bottle as regularly as he was breathing, I fell asleep. It was a bad idea, but it took little effort. The grape had become an oblong lump pushing against the backs of my eyes. My last image of Hamilton was of him stooped over the baggie as if it were an Easter basket and he a greedy-ass punk.

Sometime later Deborah must've come home, showered, then come downstairs. I woke with a shock to find her standing over me. I took a quick look around, but Hamilton wasn't in the chair anymore.

"I didn't think you were home," she said. "What stinks?"

The only thing left of Hamilton was the smell of his coat. Quickly, I checked the apartment. My wallet and keys were gone. So was my car. So was the ashtray from the coffee table. I went through the apartment again, as though maybe the keys and wallet would turn up in a corner, tied together with a note that said, 'Gotcha!'

"I was hoping to get off a little early," Deborah said, trying to ease my tension a bit, "but we got slammed at the last minute." She stood in the middle of the living room, in my way every time I passed by her. Her arms hung at her sides with helpless energy, that wanting-to-do-something-but-as-powerless-as-a-retired-marionette kind of way.

I looked out the window again, to the spot where my Toyota should have been. "Fuck me," I said. "He screwed me big time."

Deborah had a seat on the couch while I stormed around and cursed as loud as I could. Finally, she said, "You know this guy?"

That night, Deborah drove me to work. I couldn't even borrow her car since Hamilton had my license. I was given mopping detail. Shit work. Every now and then, when I swept the rag mop across another hallway into the wall, I murmured, "Fuck." Sometimes, "Dickhead." I was thinking of Hamilton and getting down on myself as well. The car was going to be the hardest to replace, but the ashtray was the thing that made me feel the worst. A con takes your wallet and your car because these are things he can use. A con takes your ashtray when he knows he can take anything he wants.

In the morning, Deborah picked me up. She was dressed for work, her apron with change pockets already tied on. Neither of us had much to say for a while. When she pulled up in front of the doors to our apartments, she said, "I'm just dropping you off. Get some sleep. I have to be in by eight."

"You're lucky," I said.

"For what?"

"You didn't get home early yesterday."

"Not much can be said for someone like that," she said. She wasn't unwise to the world, but she didn't completely follow me either. She used to go to NA not for a drug problem but because she was addicted to bad men. She'd dropped out of community college when she got engaged, but her fiancé slept around, and she broke it off when he got crabs from a hooker. One boyfriend, a muscle head who fixed motorcycles and grew his own pot, pounded on her once. Still, she had no idea what she was fortunate enough to miss. She'd only ever known people who were mildly dangerous, who could act out every now and then but never made serious trouble. She'd never known anyone dangerous and crazy both.

"Just don't play dumb," I said. "Don't say things like, 'Call the police.'"

She smiled for a bit, then stopped. "I have to get going."

I did something strange then. I touched her cheek. I didn't know if it was to comfort her or to take a good look at her face and make it real in my mind, give it dimension. I went inside and wanted a little something instead of sleeping, but Hamilton had taken the rest of that, too.

The geometry teacher called to tell me he had seen my car. This was two weeks after Hamilton's visit. "It's sitting off 561," he said. "I just drive around sometimes, and I went behind an abandoned Acme three nights ago and saw this abandoned car. Last night I saw it again and realized it was yours. I figured either you sold it or somebody hit you up for it."

"Neither," I said. "Had someone over. I was sleeping."

"Damn," he said. "So much for houseguests."

The teacher was a clean, potato-shaped sort. The time we went fishing, he asked me about being in jail. "Deb told me you'd done a little time," he said while we were baiting up our hooks. I wasn't one for prison stories, so I made it out like the military between wars—rise early, work detail, meals, down time, a movie every Friday and a lot of naps. To make sure it sounded authentic, I told him about getting into it with an armed robber named Smithy who ended up pushing my face into the gate. The teacher listened intently to every word. He probably thought I was the something sinister that made his life interesting.

"How far is the car from here?" I asked. I figured Hamilton was long gone by then, the car safe to approach.

"It'll take half an hour tops if you get Deb to give you a ride."

"What was the name of that place again?"

"Acme. The car's out back. Might not be in showroom condition. I also thought I'd see if you wanted to take the boat out again. I could have a free weekend next week."

Fishing with the teacher had been like picking up a sword and realizing you'd been Conan in a previous life—your actions are familiar, and you remember having enjoyed this once, but your body is clumsy and alien now and not what it once was. I ended up with sunburn and an empty bait box.

"We'll see," I said. "I work weekends. How'd you find the car in the first place?"

"I'm not sleeping well lately myself."

I'd never told Deborah much about Hamilton or other incarcerates I wouldn't want her to meet, and only now did she seem bothered by this. Maybe the thing with Hamilton had given her a good idea of what my life had been like before her, what kind of monsters I spent time with.

Deborah liked telling me over and over that I simply had to stay away from that life to keep on track. I couldn't always tell if she was saying this for my benefit or hers.

Something was itching at me too. Staying straight was becoming more of a chore. I had even less patience for Deborah's help. She'd once threatened not to take me to work unless I was ready on time. I kicked a dent in my wall, ended up walking to work, and showed up an hour late. When she left me a post-it note on my bedroom mirror to remind me of my appointment with my caseworker, I crumpled it up, went upstairs and threw it in her face. I could have shoved her when she came back to me with, "You want to come out on top of this, don't you?"

The night the teacher called, I tried to get Deborah to drive me out to get my car. She said she was tired from a long shift, and she said we could go get it Thursday when we both had off. I looked her in the eyes and said, "No wonder you got smacked."

"You fuck," she said. She punched me in the shoulder again and again. "You just like keeping stuff from me. You just don't want me to be a part of your life."

"Whatever," I said. What life is there to be a part of? I wanted to say.

"You fuck," she said. She went back to her place and stomped around up there for a while. I banged on the ceiling with a folding chair until my arms got tired, then I had a beer and watched The Weather Channel and glared up at the ceiling every now and then.

After a couple days, Deborah cooled off. "I moved in upstairs," she said in a phone call from her apartment, "and I'm not going to give it all up over you saying something you know you shouldn't have." I agreed, promised to never say such a thing again, and the next night we had pork lo mein and Jim Bean at my place. On Thursday we went to get my car. I sang along with the Boss on the radio to make her smile —"Jersey Girl." I told her I was gonna take that ride, and I took her hand. We hadn't gone out together like this in a long time. My best chance was that it wasn't going to be my car at all and that it would turn up later in a more promising place. But if it was, I didn't think there was going to be much to do without the keys. It wasn't going to matter anyway.

The car was wide open. The windows were down as if to air it out. "Jesus," Deborah said, and we were still ten feet away. The odor made me wince. She hung back while I surveyed the scene.

This kind of damage could have come only from a week of concerted effort. The insides of both windshields were smeared with dry mustard, ketchup, maybe even duck sauce, swirled together like finger painting. The front passenger seat was pushed forward, its back crusted with mud. The seat behind it was muddy too. The other seat in the back had blood and other stains, Slim Jim wrappers and an empty Stroehmann's bread bag. Pint-sized Chinese food cartons were stuck to the upholstery. The car smelled like old piss. There was also that heavy street stench Hamilton had left in my plush chair. The ammonia-like stink of crack smoke too. On the floor was a sheet of tin foil shaped into a pipe. Liquor bottles, various sizes. Torn-out pages from an old *Cheri* magazine. The dashboard was all cut up—"Fuck fuck fuck fuck" from door to door. Hamilton had gone ahead and thrown up on the driver's seat—probably his final move, a way of signing his work. In the dried mess I could see my license.

"How bad is it?" Deborah asked.

I kicked the car door. Hamilton had known exactly where to go to find his old prison buddy gone straight. I couldn't turn him away, but I had trouble if I let him in. And no matter where I went, he knew how to find me. As long as I had a record and stuck to the rules, I had a current address on file somewhere. Hamilton was on his own, however, out there on the move in someone else's car now. Maybe he was parked in a field, lighting up a rock. If he didn't have a whore getting high with him, he was thinking about jerking off. Go ahead and wipe off on the upholstery—what the fuck's the difference?

Things had been different on the inside. I'd get Hamilton his nacho chips and his sugar packets filled with weed. If anyone messed with me, Hamilton put out reminders that I was part of his crew, untouchable, but he never tried anything unseemly with me. Even the time he threw me off the bleachers in the recreation yard for smoking up one of his sugar packets, I knew I had it coming. You knew where you stood with him. On the outside, Hamilton did whatever he took a fancy of doing. Your only chance was that you didn't tick him off and make it worse for yourself. All I had to hope for now was that he was out doing something that was going to get him put away again soon.

"How bad?" Deborah asked again.

"Bad," I told her. "It's all really fucked."

I took the tags and everything that was mine out of the glove compartment. I peeled my license from the driver's seat and threw it into the nearby trees. Getting another license seemed better than cleaning off Hamilton's crusted puke. I figured it was best not knowing if there was anything in the trunk.

When we got back into Deborah's car, she took a long look out the window at my heap, as if she were saying goodbye.

We stopped at a nearby Denny's. I ordered a hamburger, but I only munched on a couple of fries. Deborah had a girly salad and didn't seem pleased with our waitress. She waited for the check before she started saying what she must have been preparing for an hour.

"I know this must look like things are going bad," she said. "But you're trying. You're trying hard and there are always going to be setbacks. They only feel bad because staying straight means something to you now."

I sat there shaking my head. Did she think she was Nancy Reagan?

"It's nothing worth giving up over," she said, "if that's what you're thinking."

Deborah went for a cigarette. I thought of taking her lighter and holding it up to my arm. It was the trick I had done to join Hamilton's crew, the one that showed him I was a crazy fuck worth keeping around. Sometimes he had me burn myself just so he could look into my eyes. The best part, Hamilton had said, was the eyes. He said it looked as though some stinking kind of creature was in there ready to pounce, and if it wasn't planning on hurting you, it was going to give you a hell of a scare. Deborah deserved to know exactly what it was she was getting into.

THE HUNT

The old man wants me to call him Mugsy, and the first time I do, he smiles to himself, as if I've just confirmed something he's been waiting for:

"Looks cozy, Mugsy."

It's not much of a place—two rooms, including the bathroom that is just a little bigger than a closet—but it's more space than I'm used to. I have no plans to stay very long, and the house is not connected to Mugsy's.

Mugsy rubs his chin, stubble scraping audibly. His breath smells of cigars, and the stain between the fingers on his right hand also advertises his habit. A retiree like him, or anyone for that matter who can devote himself so long to one thing to retire from it, deserves at least a cigar a day. "Yeah, it's small," he says. In some ways, Mugsy acts like my father. They bear no resemblance, except maybe in age, but Mugsy has that way about him, an air of being in the same room with a young man. "No room to do any cooking, but you can take meals in the house with me and Edna." Of course his wife's name is Edna. I imagine she'll look like one—kindly, a constant look of worry on her face, just a bit younger than Mugsy but not much. I heard her call out to Mugsy when he told her through the kitchen window that he was showing someone the guesthouse. Edna said she had a cake in the oven, ready to fall, and she'd be out in a jiffy. All I could see through the screen was a dark shape moving about. She called Mugsy 'Robert.'

Mugsy points to a corner of the room, past the sofa bed. "Cable hookup, but we don't get any movie stations. We won't pay for anything like that."

The place smells of rain and a litter box. There's an air of assurance about Mugsy, a sense of knowing where he is, where he's always going to be, making him nothing like Dad at all. Mugsy has a mole under his chin, just above the collar. Three stiff hairs grow from it, sharp and menacing in appearance, curved symmetrically away from each other. When Mugsy rubs the stubble on his chin, sometimes he strays over to the mole and fingers it, as if making sure it's still there. The hairs barely move against the force of his fingertips. The guesthouse is in the back yard, hidden from the street. It would take a conscious effort, deliberate trespassing, for anyone on the street to get even a glimpse at it. Edna has a multitude of clotheslines around the yard as well. When they are all filled, I imagine, my place will be invisible even to the main house. As he looks around the guesthouse, Mugsy pushes his Royals cap to the back of his head, and he smiles emptily for a moment, as if reminiscing.

"Looks good." I count out two months' rent, almost all of my money, but I don't let Mugsy see this. I keep my body between him and my open wallet.

"No loud music after ten," Mugsy says when the rent is in his pocket. "If Edna's cats should come sneaking in, just throw something, a shoe. Supper is five-thirty sharp." He holds out his hand, and I drop my duffel bag to take it. Mugsy squeezes, and I squeeze back, and it's a contest for a moment, but I give first and let Mugsy squeeze my fingers together. He reaches over with his other hand and pats me on the arm, just above the triceps.

"If you're looking for work, there should be plenty in town, with school starting again," he says. He hands me the key, which feels cool and sharp in my palm, and he turns and leaves me be.

*

Days, I head out and follow the want ads. Edna and Mugsy are the type who wouldn't mind me walking through the house on my way to the street, but I walk around the side of the house anyway. I like it best when Edna sees me off. She's a little shorter than I expected, a little more plump, but all the more pleasant. She wipes her hands on her apron and asks me if I want a sandwich to take, which I decline, but I wave back pleasantly. When it's Mugsy, he just points at me through the window while he's cleaning a shotgun or reading one of his hunting magazines. Despite his apparent wakefulness, there is always a sense of monotony about him. I nod back and move on. They've never both caught me leaving. All that friendliness would make me think I'm being set up.

I don't know the bus routes, so I walk. I pay attention to the numbers on the buses that pass me, but I have yet to make any sense of them. The cheapest food I can find are grilled cheese sandwiches, $1.15 at the Eckerd's lunch counter, and they stay well enough in your pocket so you can nibble on them throughout the day. I try a hardware store, a card corner, a garage. When I'm asked to fill out an application, I take it politely and leave. My jacket is full of applications, folded into eighths, heaps becoming as hard as cigarette packs. A high school dropout, a dishonorable discharge from the Air Force for cursing out a lieutenant, among other things—hardly a list of qualifications. I consider changing my strategy. At the Blue Fontaigne Diner, I consider hauling all the trash bags lying out back into the dumpster. Then I'll tell the manager how easy it was to do and push for an instant hire without paperwork. But with the door to the kitchen open, employees in their sad polyester uniforms stealing glances at me as I pass, I back down.

I come home with my feet threatening blisters, my denim jacket soaked at the armpits and a decreasing line down my back, my shoulders heavy from being under the sun so long. Edna waves, says, "Hi, Stan," but I always think she is frowning at me sympathetically. She is the kind of person who would gladly drive me into town and let me walk back, but she never offers. Sometimes I have to duck around her sheets and pillowcases to get to my place.

"We have ham tonight," she'll call out. "Biscuits and peas with corn," or, "I'm just finishing a bowl of potato salad," but I tell her I've got applications to fill, and always I pat one of my solid pockets, though I'm usually lost behind her clean laundry by then.

At five, I make sure I'm out of sight. Edna sometimes calls my name as dinner grows closer, but at five-thirty they're at the table without me. Then I open the door and sit in the jamb. Sometimes I hear clinks and scrapes, the hint of fractured conversation, but only just barely. I like the smell of evenings here, that whiff of everything starting to cool down.

Nights, I go through Mugsy and Edna's back door and take the plate they leave for me in their refrigerator. I would knock at first, but Mugsy always called out, "It's open," a dangerous habit, and I gradually got used to letting myself in. I move easily in the dark. To turn on the kitchen light seems a violation, since Mugsy and Edna watch their *Wheel of Fortune* with the lights off. I wrap the food in a napkin and leave the plate itself in the sink. I take one of their forks with me, since I have my own knife. When I have seven of their forks, I bring them back, wash them and leave them to dry in the dish rack. Mugsy and Edna's house smells of the elderly, a pungent smell, and the kitchen is complete with flowery wallpaper and pictures of babies and young kids, old and recent, in ovular frames. One photo is of a young man in Marine dress, hair high and tight, a grin threatening to crack his face open, though the picture is slightly yellowed. All four of Edna's cats linger hopefully around my feet as I scope the kitchen in refrigerator light one more time to make sure there's nothing to trip over, and I cup some water in my hand for a quick drink before leaving.

After eating, I ration myself a swallow of vodka from the fifth I keep in my bag, and I allow myself a cigarette. I sit in the dark, the sofa bed still folded away, and I count how many days until the rent is due. My cigarettes will last until then, if I keep myself to one a night. As I calculate, I click open my penknife. I watch the blade gleam in the moonlight. I shut it again. I keep the door open and let night breeze and crickets in. Out of habit, I consider how long I can put off Mugsy and Edna, how long before I will sneak out during the night. An E8 bus, I think, will get me a good distance away, maybe out by a highway. From there I'll move on. When I close my eyes I can see the road of stars some call the Milky Way. When I leave, I'll once again look at that road as my guide.

Some nights, despite the chill from fall starting up, Mugsy comes outside in boxers and a T-shirt, smoking a cigar. His posture is slumped: he looks weary of having gotten through another day, of having to face another. He walks around in the grass, which is getting long, and he stares down at his feet as he lightly stomps about. I see him touch his mole again—I know its place by heart, have had dreams about it being much larger than in real life. I suck my cigarette cautiously, when his back is turned, so he won't see the cherry. It's like he's performing a tribal dance.

I'm on my way to town when a faded red Datsun pulls over and picks me up. I wasn't asking, but when I get up to it the driver leans over and opens the passenger side for me.

"I see you along here often," he says in greeting. His hair is slicked down as though he works in a barber shop. The car shimmies in the dirt slightly before it gets back onto the road.

"I live down there." I motion back to the house. I haven't gotten more than a half-mile. Edna may still be watching me from her dining room.

"Edna and Mugs?" The man checks his rearview. He's beating the steering wheel to the radio, which I can barely hear. "Mugs used to be a builder, you know. Construction." The way he puts it makes it sound like a warning.

"I'm in the guest house," I say, and though I'm being cautious, I figure he already knows it's in the back. I fumble awkwardly; I always have trouble finding the seat belt in old cars.

"They'll take care of you, those two." He checks the rearview again, as if he thinks he can catch Edna giving him an appreciative grin. "Ask Mugs to show you some of his decoys."

"They make me dinner every night," I volunteer.

"I'd imagine."

The car engine is easier to make out than the song on the radio, but the man is still smacking out a beat.

"Where you headed?" he asks.

"Town."

I keep the front door closed and spread out my collection of applications on the floor: twenty-six in all. I didn't think there were that many businesses in town. Around lunchtime, Edna comes to my door and invites me over for tuna fish. I am nervous about all the blank applications and her just inches away, blocked only by wood with peeling paint. "Maybe later," I tell her. She promises to leave me a plate in the fridge, and she leaves and talks across the fence with Pauline next door for a while before going in to finish her tuna. Pauline is probably fifteen years younger than Edna. Black hair, grayed in the curls, overweight. She looks like somebody's aunt. She sometimes hangs out her clothes with her blouse off, as if maybe she doesn't know I can see into her yard, which has grass as long as Mugsy's. Maybe she does know, though she has only ever smiled at me in a neighborly way. Everyone in the neighborhood seems to know me—people lift their hands from their steering wheels when they pass. No one walks around here. At best, they raise their hands while on their porches, or nod at me while reaching into their mailboxes. The mailman will say things like, "Great day," as he hurries past me along his route.

Despite myself, I've figured on some places I can root around for cash, loose change, maybe even jewelry, in Edna and Mugsy's living room. I've picked obvious spots: the ashtrays on the mantle, the jackets that hang on the closet door, the blue ceramic jars with yellow flowers, laden with a single, defenseless-looking bee, that are lined in order of size on the kitchen counter. Places that I can search quickly, move through quietly, requiring no light. I can imagine Edna looking a little shook up, dismayed, Mugsy toying with his mole in an agitated manner, both angry, a little upset, feeling violated, but mostly disappointed and spreading their disappointment all over the neighborhood, everyone thinking about me with disapproving frowns.

While on my way to Beefsteak Charlie's, though I figure I'll have little chance there even if I did fill out an application, a plumber who was looking for an assistant leans out the front door of his shop and asks me, "Did you ever get that form back to me?" The way he asks me is earnest, in no way an accusation, though I take it as such anyway.

"Tuesday," I say, fearing for a moment that it is Tuesday, but it isn't, and I keep walking the way I do past all the places I've never gotten back to—straight ahead, inconspicuous, just a passerby.

Back home, I pull Mugsy's lawn mower out of the shed. It obviously needs work: the blades rusty, the axle clogged with neglect and grass. I have fifteen days before the rent money I gave Mugsy runs out, and I root through Mugsy's hedge clippers and hose and old bags of fertilizer until I find WD-40. I go at the mower blades with it, wiping off rust with one of my own T-shirts. Edna comes out and tells me to put the shirt right in the washer when I'm done. Her tone is casual, but still I expect her to call Mugsy out into the yard and point me out to him. In the end, my work is shoddy at best—I can't get all the rust off the blades, have no idea how to sharpen them, but I get the axle turning at least after I scrape out most of the grass jammed in there. I allow myself two cigarettes while I work, regretting them immediately, both for cheating on my ration and letting Mugsy and Edna see my habit, though I like the feel of the sun on my back now, and Edna even brings me iced tea, which tastes good in the thick, clear plastic cup.

It takes me the rest of the afternoon to mow one strip of the back yard. The slightest bit of grass jams the axle, and I have to clear it out all over again. Also, the blades hardly cut, and I have to run over the same stretch of grass over and over until the axle jams again. I imagine Edna and Mugsy are checking up on me time and again, though I see nothing of them until dinner, which I eat outside on the back stoop, while listening through the dining room windows to Edna telling Mugsy about a Mrs. Fielding and her cat that will only eat canned food with heart in it.

It takes me three days to finish the back yard. The mower feels pretty broken-in, and by leaning into it hard when I push, I've found a way of getting it around more easily. I have to practically throw myself at the handles to make it move like a regular mower. I use Mugsy's hedge clippers to trim the edges by the fence, and when Edna has things out on the line, I make it into a game, a dance really, of ducking under the sheets and bedspreads, swerving past Mugsy's tank tops. When their underwear is out, I make it a point to mow in different areas. I've even started letting Edna wash my things, and when I pass them, shifting slightly in the breeze, I run the fabrics briefly between my fingers to see if they're dry yet. Though I was used to the smell of my clothes after several wearings, I now appreciate more the smell of being washed in Edna's lemon-scented detergent and dried by midwestern air.

Mugsy comes out and views my work after I am done. He has been away in his den ("Cooped up," Edna calls it), polishing his guns, finishing the decoys, now that duck season opens soon, and Edna and I pull down the laundry so Mugsy can get a good view. I even run the hose a minute to make the lawn glisten.

Mugsy chews on the stub to a Phillie thoughtfully. I expect him to step off the back stoop, maybe even check one of the grass blades for length, but the time he puts into studying the layout of the yard satisfies me that he's taking this seriously.

"Looks good," he concedes. "Damn fine."

*

Mugsy finally brings up rent over dinner. "Potatoes," he asks, and after I pass him the bowl, after a silence filled only by the wet sound of serving spoon meeting mashed potato, he says, "Rent's in a few days."

I've prepared for this moment, but still my words come out awkward, unrehearsed, with a stammer.

"Haven't heard a word," I say. "I've been around, but no one's called back."

Edna looks at Mugsy with an exaggerated frown, as if this is something the two of them have discussed, and Mugsy turns up one corner of his mouth.

"I thought Applebaum needed someone to sweep his floor," Mugsy says.

This time, lying is a fearful action. I've heard about small towns, where everyone knows everyone else's business, the perfect places to avoid, but I go ahead and do it anyway, "He doesn't seem to want me for it," and hope for the best.

Mugsy only stares into his food. "Goddamn Applebaum," he says. "I was ready to punch him when he fired that black boy."

"Nelson," Edna finishes for him.

There is an unrestful silence.

"Pauline next door needs her back yard done," he says, finally. "I can find some other things for you to do around here." Edna only grins, but she doesn't hide her excitement easily. I smile back and nod apologetically.

Pauline makes me nervous, the way she watches me while I work. She's asked Mugsy if I would do the lawn again, though it's only been two weeks and the mower hardly picks up anything. The way she watches me is different from the way Mrs. Dugan down the street does—Mrs. Dugan collects lawn jockeys (some white, some night black with large, red lips, some with lanterns, some without, one even with the right arm broken off entirely), and she watched me intently, as if to make sure I did no damage to her collection. Once she even called out to me, "Don't go running your wheels into that one," referring to one so old the once red equestrian jacket was just stone with random flakes left, "or he'll tip."

While I work, Pauline likes to compliment my efforts. "Mugsy couldn't make that thing budge," or, "It's amazing how much grass that picks up. Roger Morton, the one in the yellow house with white shutters, he has one of those power jobs, but it jams the second it hits twigs or anything like that." Whenever she offers me a cold drink, she invites me inside for it, and though I follow almost right behind her, I expect every time to go in and find her backed up against her kitchen counter, her house coat open, her chubby waist pinched up under one of her numerous large, pink panties, the kind she keeps out on the line while I work. I see the way her eyes come up whenever I turn to face her, and inside her house I drink quickly and go back to work.

I've done almost half the lawns in the neighborhood, and by now I can call most of the neighbors by name. Mugsy is like my supervisor, giving me a list of jobs every morning while Edna serves me breakfast. I repeat his instructions word for word, military style, my voice muffled by eggs or a mouthful of cranberry muffin and orange juice. I've also cleaned out Mugsy's tool shed, replaced one of the fence posts, regrouted the bathtub. Mugsy has taken to doing his work outside when I'm out there. When he's cleaning his guns, he'll look at me through the barrel, as if watching me through a telescope. His collection of decoys is a fine one. Under scrutiny, it's easy to tell they're wood, but scanning past them, you wouldn't be surprised if one of the heads suddenly cocked to the side and quacked reflectively. Mugsy's flock is even well selected to look convincing—there are only a few females, brown and cloistered, at least two mallards hovering competitively around each.

What is most intriguing is the care Mugsy takes with them. While outside, he touches them up, repainting the heads with great care, adding red for a lifelike glow. Though I try to compliment him on them, their exquisite work and beauty, Mugsy merely nods as if I'm bothering him and I recede, embarrassed. Sometimes, while he works, Mugsy will blurt out advice:

"Wood's the only way to go, Stan. Some say it comes off too shiny, but not if you treat it right." He holds up the one he's working on. He revolves it in the sun to prove his point. "Plastic's just too dull. Makes a mallard look too much like a bath toy." At this, I laugh like it's a good joke I'll want to tell others.

To make the mowing jobs easier, I've considered asking Mugsy for a bike, a three-speed maybe, used, or even one of those old one-speeds that you brake with the pedals, and attaching it to the mower. I have this all planned out in my head. If I attach the mower to the front, and it jams, I'll go right over the handlebars. I'd normally get very little cutting power at all if the mower's attached to the back, but I've considered also asking Mugsy for some iron plates I can bungee to the frame to weigh the mower down. One day, Mugsy bought me a carton of cigarettes, Pall Malls, though I smoke Kool, for all the work I had done, he told me, and because I seemed to be out. I took them with reservations, but I took them. I can only keep this act up for about a month and a half. Any longer, and they'll only think I was a freeloader when I leave in the middle of the night. Otherwise, I hope they'll consider me a hard-luck case, an unfortunate, leaving behind a misfit contraption—a mower attached to a bicycle—to remind them.

Today, Mugsy's moved all of his hunting equipment out into the yard: four shotguns, a knife that's long and dangerous-looking, his string of decoys and his hunting outfit: neon red cap with earflaps, flannel coat with shaggy lining, abrasive-looking waterproof pants, fishing boots. The coat is gargantuan. It's three sizes too big for him, and for a moment I consider that maybe Mugsy keeps his kills under it, pressed up against his sides, to keep them warm until he gets home. I'm up early because Mugsy told me the night before he had some early work for me to do, and now it's six in the morning, and Mugsy is here outside in his long johns getting dressed.

"Edna's sleeping," he whispers as I shiver in the morning air. He motions up to their bedroom window. In a moment, I see why Mugsy has to dress outside—he grunts and curses his way into his pants, which must be from an earlier, lighter time. I smoke a Pall Mall for warmth as I watch. I decided the night before that it would be only fair to tell Mugsy and Edna that I have to leave, but Mugsy is far too active this early in the morning, and I'm still far too groggy to make such an announcement.

"I wore this outfit every day for a while," Mugsy tells me, sitting on the stoop as he works hard to button his pants. "Edna decided that hunting was an immoral thing and that I shouldn't do it anymore, so I wore the whole sh-bang every day, cap and all, all season long for three years, because I wanted to be ready the moment she changed her mind." He smiles at me, an unlit stogie in the corner of his mouth. His pants on, suspenders up, he starts into his coat. "We'll be on our way any second now, Stan," he says, though I expect him to call me something else, a name more endearing, maybe. His hand on the back of my neck when he leads me over to his equipment is stiff, rough, clutching, almost painful.

We go out to a marsh Mugsy says always has a good roost. His guns are stacked along the back window of his truck. Though Mugsy smoked the whole ride over, I've kept the windows closed because of the cold, and I feel somewhat lightheaded when we finally stop and get out. Mugsy apparently sees my discomfort, and he says, "You think you cigarette smokers got it bad—even you hate cigar smoke!" He's more excited than I've ever seen him, and his earflaps are tied so tight under his chin that I expect to see his face start losing color. He puts his hand on my shoulder as I get his guns off the rack for him. "Be easy," he says, "be easy. No need to let the honkers know what we're doing." Mugsy's words are instructive and without criticism.

We are in luck—already I can hear Canadian geese approaching. Mugsy takes the long double barrel and I haul the rest of his equipment in a large, green sack that's almost too much for me to carry. I wonder how many other people Mugsy has gotten to do this for him.

We skulk through the grass, cautiously but hurriedly, for the geese are getting closer. They are close enough for us to make out their V-formation under whisping cirrus. My sneakers are getting muddy and camouflaged by threads of the marsh grass that is almost cotton-like to the touch, but I keep my pace, right behind Mugsy, who is moving like a teenager, though he's already breathing heavy. When we reach his crouch, I consider telling him right then and there that I can't stay anymore, that I appreciate everything him and Edna have done for me, and I even decide that I should make things look good by offering to send him the back rent as soon as I can, but the geese are virtually overhead now, and Mugsy checks over his shotgun one more time before aiming it up at the sky.

The gun goes off—a pop, really, of a few dozen firecrackers going off at the same time—and immediately afterward, so soon that you might have thought the bird was hit before the gun even went off, a goose plummets toward the marsh.

"Watch it fall," Mugsy instructs. I hear the geese honking all the louder, in desperation probably, and I can imagine them flapping their wings quickly now, flight their only hope, but I watch the shot goose disappear into the spread of grass in front of me.

"Go, go," Mugsy shouts, "go get 'em." I take off in a sprint in the direction of the fallen goose. Instinctively, I go for my knife, though it's small and not very sharp at all, because a dying creature can be very dangerous, and as I'm running, I hear another shot go off, and Mugsy shouts out, "Coming down. To your left, your left." I hear the click of the shotgun being opened, and I want Mugsy to reload as quickly as he can, because I'm running fast. I figure that, with my speed, puddles and soft spots in the ground will be easy to run over, and I believe I can even smell the goose as I come closer: a stink of wet feathers, wounded flesh, gunpowder. I want Mugsy to keep firing, because there's a glorious little grunt he makes when his gun is about to go off, in anticipation of the recoil that will press into his shoulder, and I want geese to keep falling, for when I come across the first one, nestled deep in an impression of grass, twisted and grotesque and dead, I grab it with little regard for the blood and I hold it up for Mugsy. I expect him to be watching me with pride, but he's busy with his gun, looking between it and the sky, and he's shouting, "Go get the goose to your left. Go get it," so I start off the for the next one, and it is the rediscovered joy of running, limp goose wings waving about with me, brushing against my jeans, that I want to savor and continue with, and for Mugsy I think I could run like this for hours.

ARTISTIC ENDEAVOR

In the midst of our cuddle on his living room couch, Mike takes my hand. A Venus fly trap devouring a chigger— my fingertip can barely cover one of his weightlifting calluses. Mike somehow manages the edge of his pipe-thick thumb between the bones leading to my middle and ring fingers.

"It's a ch'i spot," Mike says as he pushes down. His thumb presses apart my knuckles. "This is going to hurt something awful."

It isn't long before I feel the urge to pull away, but Mike's hands are strong and he has me tight. He presses harder. To shut out the image of compound fractures and reconstructive surgery, I stare into the scars on his hand, the pink tracks from barbed wire and the puncture dots that look like burst pimples.

"Just make like there's no pain," he says. "This is nothing. Try not noticing a fence staple while it's getting plucked out of your hand."

Mike is a performance artist, a professional wrestler to the uninformed. To pay the bills he trains well-off slugs with sedentary lifestyles, but once a month he and his mortal enemy, his former tag-team partner gone bad (or vice versa), fight with cheese graters, with baseball bats wrapped in barbed wire. They fight with flaming fold-up chairs, with fence staplers. They dress the same and dye their hair the same color so no one can tell them apart. There is no hero, no villain—no one to root for. The crowd cheers solely for the violence itself. Videos of his matches are big on YouTube and in Japan, but Mike won't let me watch one. We've only been seeing each other two weeks, and he wants me to experience one of his shows first-hand.

He wiggles his thumb as though attempting some kind of massage.

"He does this to his own girlfriend," Mike says, meaning his opponent. "He says it keeps down her urges." Mike abstains for three days before a show. He says the build-up heightens the performance.

"A broken hand would definitely cool my jets," I say through my teeth.

He presses even harder a moment to show me he's been holding back. "You're a fragile one," he says. "I could've popped your arm out already if I were so inclined." He gives my hand a slight jerk. "Clunk," he says, and he smiles.

Mike has a good smile—warm and sexy. His gray eyes gleam when he is showing off his strength. Odd to think I'm on the verge of jumping the bones of a man about to break my hand into two distinct halves, but the idea is there just the same.

"Maybe I'll go back to my place," I say.

"Weren't you there just yesterday?" Mike pulls in his lips, ready to make this a fight. He leans in over me as though ready to block my escape.

"I can scream," I say.

"I'll silence you," he says. "I'll break you into submission and keep you under wraps until I'm ready for you."

I laugh, but I'm only getting hotter.

"Uncle," I say.

"You're damn right, uncle." Mike considers my hand, from there looks over every inch of me, then lets me leave. The back of my hand has a wide, red spot already tingling of bruise. In the elevator going down, I avoid eye contact with a scruffy man in a dirty pullover and an older woman who doesn't look like she gets out much. I feel guilty of some crime.

Martha must know how I sound when I'm trying to sneak past her floor on the way to my own. That, or she's been poking her head in and out of her apartment half the night.

"Are you all right?" she says as she marches up to me. She puts out her hand, as though she expects me to need assistance.

"Sleepy, but fine," I say. I continue up the stairs, but she comes along beside me, visually inspecting me for the battering she's convinced Mike is going to give me one day. I keep the end of my sleeve over my hand the rest of the way up the stairs, but I drop my guard when I unlock my apartment door. My bruise, now full-fledged, probably glints like opal to her critical eye.

"I told you, Karen," Martha says. She stomps right into my one-room apartment and has a seat by my bed. She crosses her arms and puts on her Let's Talk About It face, but I just want to sleep.

"He gave me a deep muscle massage is all," I say. "People pay a hundred bucks for thirty minutes of the same treatment." I close the door, then take off my shirt. I hide my hand behind my back as I undo my bra.

Martha keeps her game face at full force. "Deep muscle massage," she says. "The kind the secret police use just before they resort to hot pokers." Martha's known me since we were cashiers in a bagel shop—me a scared art student new to the City, smuggling poppy seed and everything in my waistband come quitting time, Martha toting a fresh Masters from NYU and out to convince someone she'd make a good editor. She claims she can smell bullshit as easily as a pot of fresh Ethiopian.

Before I take off my glasses, I look at myself, down to my panties, in the mirror on the closet door.

"He's a fine-tuned machine," I say. "And I'm all soft and puffy. He would have barely noticed the same amount of pressure." I get into bed and wiggle all the way under the covers. When I look up, I can see a glow of light coming through the sheet. When I look down, it is as though I am not there.

Out there, beyond the walls of my cocoon, Martha says, "That man has invaded you like a Hun, and you've already given him access to the Citadel. He knows you're a sculptor, and he gets all stigmata on your hand. Tell me at least you're still working on your boxes."

I hesitate, trying to find a positive way to say, "Not for a couple of weeks," but Martha's chair is creaking before I can think of something. I make shoebox-sized wood sculptures. Each one its own universe: couples foxtrotting under mauve palm trees with a bowl of Wheaties as a backdrop, that kind of thing. I have a whopping five of them currently on display in some back room gallery I haven't even seen yet.

"He's in my next one," I say, finally. "I'm just doing research."

Martha was with me when I first met Mike. We were checking out a gym and its clientele. Mike and his partner were tossing a seventy-pound dumbbell back and forth with practiced rhythm. Martha thought they could have been twins, but I knew which one I wanted. He was the one who looked at his partner with a slight alpha-male smirk each time he caught the weight. There was also something I liked instantly about the way he wiped at his sweat as though angry with it. When his partner went for a heavier dumbbell, I introduced myself. He seemed more annoyed than anything to meet me, but I kept pressing even when Martha was trying to pull me away. When I told him I was a wood sculptor, he said, "That's a lot of sitting around, isn't it?"

"Jesus, Martha," I say. "This is just my hand. Imagine how it feels to dive backwards through a table from ten feet up." The darkness under the blankets keeps my hand from hurting too much.

Martha responds so quickly I know she's been waiting for the right opportunity to say this: "Karen, you should have maced him in the face the second he started busting up your hand. Being safe is ninety-nine percent prevention, picking up on the warning signs and acting on them before they get worse. If you find yourself in a bad situation, you've already failed—the trick then becomes to get yourself out before you become a trophy on the wall." Martha has all these principles because she's been through a couple of bad situations herself. Every Tuesday night, she and other renounced victims kick dummies and scream dissent from the diaphragm. Some Tuesdays they get to kick a volunteer in padding that makes him look like sumo. She brought me in for Bring a Sister night, but the guy in the suit was a laugh. As if he had much concern for the kind of damage a girl could do to him.

"I need my beauty sleep," I tell Martha. I throw the covers down to show her I'm serious. Martha holds her ground for a bit, then finally stands and makes sure I see that her feelings are hurt before she starts for the door.

I let her get her hand on the knob before I say, "I know how to take care of myself. Let's drink too many margaritas soon, on me."

Martha turns back. "Tell me precisely when."

"Not tomorrow," I say. "You can guess why." I bury myself under the covers again before she can give me one of those disappointed stares.

In the morning, my hand is plenty stiff. A spot in the middle of my palm hurts when I bend my fingers. The bruise is like looking into a storm cloud from above—an inky black mass with streaks and spots of purple. It is 8 a.m., and I know Mike is in his kitchen, separating the yolks out of three extra-large eggs. He eats eight times a day, every bite scheduled to his metabolism. He weighs his food. I picture his arms making curling motions as he coaxes the whites into the blender. Watching him mix his 9:45 a.m. yogurt with grapes, granola and 4 oz. of banana is like watching a ballerina warm up. I put a mug of yesterday's coffee in the microwave and run cold water over my hand.

Martha says you can learn a lot about me from my hands—precision, a natural talent for fine arts, that kind of crap. She says ancient Mediterranean cultures would have had festivals to celebrate my latest works, but I find that about as likely as someone yelping like a run over dog at a gallery show and going home to tell his friends of this kick-ass wood sculpture they just *got* to see for themselves. When Mike first saw one of my pieces, his reaction was as blank as white paint. It was the one I have mounted over my sink: a pyramid of green army men assembled before a river of braided Halloween garlands, black bats and witches abroom poking up like crests and waves. Fiery wisp-like creatures I made by chopping the hair off a dozen Troll dolls ride the currents.

I can think of the steps I took in making this monstrosity, how the snipers looked like a good foundation to build up from and how the pyramid created the need for an audience and how good it felt to cut the blue and orange hair from those stupid, stupid dolls—but what good was any this effort but to make art intellectuals like Martha give thoughtful nods and engage in critical analysis in a way loud enough to let others appreciate their smarts?

When I know Mike is finished drinking his protein shake, I call.

"How's the hand?" he says.

"Bruised."

"Is that it?"

"It hurts some when I move my fingers."

"A deep bruise, at least."

"Satisfied?"

"I should have kept you around while I did my nighttime calisthenics. You could've slapped my abs while I did crunches."

His exquisite musculature is all part of his performance— the horror of an electrified barbed wire match juxtaposed with two tanned, firm specimens of male perfection. With this kind of intensity in the world, what chance does a piece of shit box sculpture have? I hear Mike cut apart an apple, put it on the scale a moment, then spread soy butter on the slices. My coffee tastes like there's Seran Wrap keeping me from its full flavor. Mike tells me I can't come over tonight because he has to meditate on the beating he's going to be taking.

"The sensation you call pain," he says, "is surprise, the nerve endings suddenly deluged with a torrent of impulses. So I anticipate the worst. I prepare to have my ear ripped off by a strip of barbed wire, so when all I get is a harsh yank with a nutcracker, I barely notice it happened."

"I guess I'll have to spend the evening with Martha," I say. Mike is quiet a moment, clearly trying to remember who Martha is.

Then, out of the blue he says, "So how's the sculpting?"

I take a moment to find the words that will say what I mean. "I used to like it," I say, "like doing it, I mean. But I'm starting to wonder the point of it." It's easy to say these kinds of things to Mike because he lets me finish my thoughts. Martha is always trying to find a response to what I say, especially if it's something negative, as though she has an allergy to self-deprecating comments and can't let them go unrefuted.

"It's been a struggle lately to get any work done," I say. "It's like walking with fat thighs, fatter than I have now."

"Then you need to skinny down," he says, of course while his mouth is full.

"So what do I do?" I say. "Shut myself away and forget to eat until I die of starvation?" I bang my mug audibly on the counter. Does that bastard think I'm drinking coffee for breakfast?

"That," Mike says, "or do a sun dance. Tearing off a nipple should inspire something. You'll see what I mean. I'm on tomorrow night, and you're on the guest list."

"He'll plead artistic endeavor," Martha says. She's waving a long, thin spoon at me menacingly. "He'll pound you into to a bag of bargain meat, then defend himself on the evening news with words like 'inspiration' and 'freedom of expression.' He'll make John Wayne Bobbit the next Laurie Anderson. While you shake and blubber at a survivor's group, the son of a bitch will get an NEA." We've started our evening at an ice cream shop. Martha treats me to a chocolate double-malted just to make sure I know what's unhealthy. After this, she wants to go back to her apartment to watch Friday night prime time. She's considered showing me *Sleeping With the Enemy* so I know there is always hope in moving on to another relationship, but who's to believe that skinny-ass Julia Roberts ever had a finger lifted against her? About as much empowerment as a fat-free Twinkie.

"He'll surely be responsible for selling out the premiere of *Beating Lorena*." Martha hacks at the brownie at the bottom of her bowl to let the Death by Chocolate seep into it thoroughly. "Funny he should advise you to slim down your thighs. Legs are the strongest part of the female body. I was going to suggest you take up kickboxing. Testicles hurt worse when you kick up rather than straight ahead."

I decide not to tell her that I'm going to Mike's next show. She would worry about me ending up like Talia Shire, embracing Rocky's battered shell after the match, promising my undying love.

"Eat up," she says, "and we'll get a movie."

"What about too many margaritas?"

"Too many margaritas it is then."

At the bar, Martha makes eyes with a couple of coffeehouse-types and entices them over. Martha tells them I'm into artists, says it like I'm free and on the make, but these boys with their stylish shirts and literary references don't look like they could write their way out of a polite yawn. I've drunk a little much, but I make a valid point anyway.

"Hot coffee in the face," I say to the one who likes to show off how he can pronounce Vladimir Nabokov's name correctly. This boy laughs as though he has the foggiest notion what I'm talking about. I turn in my stool and face him straight on. Martha gives me a look.

"Hot coffee," I reiterate. "Coffee on the plateau of boiling, multi-million-dollar-lawsuit kind of hot. And I put the whole mug; no, say the whole fucking pot in your face." I say this with a gesture and ample volume to beat out the jukebox. "Tell me what kind of reaction that'd get out of you."

"Sounds painful," the boy says.

"You'd scream like a bitch," I say. "I'd like to see your poetry do something *that* painful."

In the cab home, Martha says, "You're losing your context, kid." Two definite signs she's in lecture mode: she's calling me kid, and she's not even trying to meet my eyes. "It's like you've been reborn a pack animal, only able to relate in a competitive mode."

"I've just lost patience with pretension," I say. I say Nabokov's name a few times and make flighty hand gestures.

Martha opens the ashtray, then snaps it shut as though it's just disagreed with her. "At least they looked safe. At least they wouldn't require Navy Seal training for you to make it through a first date."

"Children," I say, countering Martha's lack of eye contact by looking out the window on my side. "Sucking on latte-flavored binkies."

"You still haven't gone to your own exhibit, have you?" Martha turns and looks at me for this one, since she knows I won't bother answering.

"Maybe someone will buy one for a bookend," I say. "Put it to some good goddamn use."

"I think your work is improving," Martha says. "Art comes from the soul, and you just need to spend some time on yours." Martha is just a copy editor who now and then writes poetry so full of Greek corpses it's indecipherable, but it's enough to let her consider herself an expert on art. The gist of what she says next is this:

Martha worries that I'm sacrificing my own identity to please Mike. She says I would be happier with someone who wants a woman who is herself, but to me that sounds like complacency, like getting stale. I say something back, something about liking the challenge of finding something new about myself. It's my summation that worries her the most.

"Even if someone has to beat out of me," I say.

The cab pulls up in front of our building, and together we pay the fare and walk up the stairs to Martha's floor. I look at Martha, and she winces as though she's expecting me to say something unkind. Her intentions may be in a good place, so I just nod farewell. I rush up the rest of the stairs and call Mike.

"I'm busy," he says. "I'm about to dive over the rope with my head caught between the rungs of an aluminum ladder. So leave me the hell alone and I'll see you tomorrow night."

I'm about to doze off when he hangs up.

The performance is at a Catholic youth center in New Jersey. It takes me three trains and a bus to get there. I am wearing black jeans, a dark blue turtleneck, and my army surplus trench coat. The preliminaries are already underway, so I take a seat in the pullout bleachers at first, away from the small crowd standing around the ring. But the bleachers hum with the stench of stale beer and old chewing gum, and who knows what I could be sitting on, so I move in amid the fans, who are mostly men of course. Though they are holding hubcaps and street signs and copper pipes, they seem quite benign. Some biker-types and guys wearing leather and spikes, even a gang of skinheads ringside, but nothing that sets off any kind of fight/flight response. To tell the truth, they all look like shoppers who have been at a flea market too long. But they do make me feel conservative—I must be the only woman not wearing a concert tee or flannel tied up against the ribs.

I make my way to a spot where I have little trouble seeing the ring. Inside, two guys in neon tights are jumping around and on top of each other. Their efforts look rehearsed and dispassionately choreographed, like a grade school dance recital. Even a backhand chop to the chest, though audible, seems to have little more impact than a movie slap. Next to me is a scrawny kid too tall for his age, his hair a mess and his goatee little more than an uneven scrape of charcoal. When he turns to me, I pretend to be interested in the dance, but he keeps staring at me, and after a while I figure it's better to let him say his piece and be done with him.

"I hate the prelims," he says, his smile full of false confidence. "A bunch of pansies trying to be Kerri Strug. I come to see the real men get it on." He nods to a box he has on the floor between his feet.

I consider blurting out to the kid that I'm banging one of his real men, but all I do is nod and hint at a smile.

The kid continues to make side comments to me now and then during the rest of the match and the one after it, which is also unremarkable for its clumsy acrobatics. His every comment questions the sexual orientations of the performers: "They should call that move 'The Cornholer,'" or "He might as well kiss the guy first."

The crowd thickens a little by the time the next preliminary ends, but still I manage to get a couple side steps away from the kid, who remains protective over his box and doesn't come after me.

The lights go down, and the crowd starts vibrating a little, moving in steady tremors. People around me who haven't already been brandishing weaponry start pulling things from concealed places. Tire irons, bicycle chains. A guy in full beard and kerchief pulls out a portable drill. Objects are passed over me and into the ring. The kid with the box reaches down and pulls out a battery-powered blender, which he turns on puree and waves over his head horror-movie style before passing it up.

Then without warning, out of the entranceway come Mike and his opponent. They have each other by the hair, and they are punching each other tempestuously. I have to weave like a sparring partner to see around the bodies hopping up and down in front of me. Mike and his opponent both have on jeans and sleeveless black Harley tees and I can't tell them apart at first. Both even have blood spread across their foreheads already. After a few roundhouse exchanges, they pull each other down the ramp towards the ring. It takes me a minute or so before I recognize the slight waddle Mike has when he walks, but by then he's through the ropes, and he and his opponent go for the weapons that have been offered up.

They start with some of the more tame items—trashcan lids, a folding chair, No Parking signs. For a while, they do nothing more than take turns whacking each other over the head. This is obviously a preamble, and I tingle tip to toe with the anticipation of something much much worse happening.

Then it's worse. The opponent shatters a fluorescent light rod over Mike's head, and Mike makes it clear to everyone that he's mad now. As the cloud of gas around him settles, he reaches for a Formica tabletop, and all hell breaks loose.

A woman up on someone's shoulders shows her fallen tits for a round of approval. The skinheads up front lock their arms together so they can move as a single mass. When Mike swings the tabletop so hard that it splits in two over his opponent's head, the mass bounces in place and chants, "Ho-ly shit! Ho-ly shit!" Their movements cause ripples, and I am suddenly being pushed from all directions. I pull my arms up against my sides and I realize how safe I've been all my life. I've felt nervous in dark alleys, dreaded the immediate prospects of my future when approached by Dahmer-looking weirdoes at bars, but being in the middle of this near-riot (at best, a mosh pit) makes my lungs feel as though they're being force fed burning marsh gas.

I instinctively look for the exit signs, but they're too far away, and I feel like a neon pink couch in a room painted black. I'm conspicuous, a target. I'm dressed all wrong. I wear glasses. Even worse, I am completely unable to get into the spirit of things. When Mike has his hand shoved into the electric blender, the kid who brought it beams as though he's just had a personal visit from Ed McMahon and the prize committee, but I'm involved. It matters to me when I see Mike get a pizza cutter rolled over his forehead because I'm the one who's going to have to look at him the next day, but I also can't seem to shake my innate need for justice. When Mike takes the portable drill and runs it a moment behind his opponent's ear, I feel he is only right—after all, he just had his nose pulled with a bolt cutter. When the opponent pours out a sack full of thumbtacks into the ring and slams Mike onto them, the guys around me groan with sympathy pain and delight, but I have a lump like putrid hardboiled egg in my colon.

In the end, there is no finality, no sense of completion. Neither man pins the other, nor attempts to do so. Mike and his opponent roll from the ring and fight their way out of sight. The people stir and chant and stomp feet for a couple minutes (I'm surprised no one holds up a Zippo), but when the house lights come up, they obediently turn and leave. The blender kid and I meet eyes, and I expect him to come onto me again, but he's had the fight taken out of him. He smiles at me in a congratulatory way, welcoming me to the club, and moves on. My arms feel as though they've been holding back boulders, and only now do I realize I've been clenching my teeth through the entire show.

When the gymnasium is almost empty, I go back to the locker rooms. I hover in the hallway between the Men's and Women's, not sure which Mike is going to come from. Guys periodically emerge from both, looking showered, their eyes to the floor. One looks at me hopefully, as though he wants me to bug him for an autograph.

Finally, Mike comes from the Men's lockers, a square of gauze taped to his forehead and a white t-back shirt despite February. There's a deep blush of red on his right shoulder, where he landed on the thumbtacks. Otherwise, he looks fresh from the gym.

"I thought you'd come out looking like a bowl of borscht with legs," I say.

Mike smiles, though with effort. "I clean up well," he says. "They keep a cut doctor on hand." He grimaces as he slings his gear bag over his good shoulder.

The locker room door opens again, and out comes Mike's opponent and his own girlfriend.

"You've met Carl," Mike says. I nod to Carl, but his nod back has a real fuck-off attitude to it. I figure it would be a bad idea to tell him it was a good show. He's wearing a neon blue tee that's a size or two too small. It makes his upper body look like a steroid detonation.

The girlfriend is standing a pace behind Carl. She is tall, even without her heels and stiff, bleached hair. She's pretty too, somewhere underneath all that makeup, and she's bright as hell—her spandex is neon, and her top could control air traffic. I'm surprised she's not snapping gum.

"That's Katrina," Mike says. I put up my hand, and Katrina turns on a smile just long enough to wave back.

"Pleasure," I say, but that's not the word I would use to describe my assessment of her. On one hand, I am glad we don't resemble each other. I would hate to think Mike has been trying to score a replica of her for himself. But coming out of tonight's testosterone fest, it would have been nice to meet a woman who looked like she could discuss something more than the best cream rinse out on the market.

Besides, I get the distinct impression that Katrina would rather be the only female along with these two guys, and it rears up my antagonism better than a cattle prod.

Carl looks right past me. "We're thinking of getting a bite," he says to Mike. "Something greasy no doubt. You in?"

Martha would have some biting reminder that she's not chopped liver, but she's never stood between these guys. Carl's biceps alone wash all want of equality right out of me. I look at Katrina, and she gives me this blank look as though she's waiting for me to do something interesting, like go away.

Mike puts his hand on my shoulder. "We're going to head back," he says. "Those thumbtacks put the hurt on me something awful."

"All part of the game, bud." Carl rubs his forehead up by his own gauze, which is closer to the hairline. "Thumbtacks hurt."

"Next time it's you," Mike says. "And it's going to be something on fire, I can assure you."

Carl smiles and laughs once like he's gotten a joke he doesn't think is all that funny. "We'll see," he says.

I don't know how I ever thought Carl and Mike looked so much alike. Carl looks like a comic book cover. Exaggerated and empty of substance. A perfect model for one of my boxes.

"Last chance to talk me into buying you a meal full of lard," Carl says. I notice he is trying to keep his weight on his right leg.

"I think Karen here wants to get home," Mike says. He leans forward, and I can feel his breath on the top of my head. "It's her first, so I'm sure she'd rather spend the rest of the night doing something a little more low-impact." He gives me a slight pat on the ass as a signal for me to comply.

"Great," I say. "Blame it on me."

Carl waits, as if the last word on this can only come from Mike. He shifts his weight momentarily, then back when his left knee buckles a bit. Finally he says, "Fine. Fuck off, and I'll see you Tuesday."

As Carl walks around Mike and me, Katrina following, Mike says, "You're getting soft if you want three days to rest up."

"Soft, soft," Carl says. He reaches back, takes Katrina's hand, and brings her alongside him. "You'll see who's soft, pal."

Off they go, towards the exit at the end of the hall, Katrina double-timing her heel-retarded steps to keep up with Carl's tired and injured lope. He lets go of her and works his hand up and down her back.

"I'm out the near door," Mike says, pushing lightly on my shoulder. "Carl thinks parking too close to the dressing rooms makes for a bad show."

We get to Mike's Honda, and he has me drive. As he clambers into the passenger seat, he favors the right side of his back.

"Katrina sure didn't want me along," I say as we pull out.

"She's a good egg." Mike is turned toward me, but it's because of his back rather than any concern for my being odd-peg-out. "She's real good for Carl. His last girlfriend never came to shows, found the whole business horrid. Katrina knows it's a big deal for him."

"Probably helps that she carries his gear bag," I say. I look into the rearview to pretend I'm not noticing Mike's glare.

"That's not all he wants," he says.

"Don't be so sure," I say. "Most guys go for a personal lackey. I didn't even know girlfriends were allowed in the locker room." My temples are tight, my hands pinching the wheel. If Mike's expecting another high-haired porter who for all I know scrubs Carl's back in the shower, I'm going to make his hurting ass walk home, even if it is his two-door I'll be kicking him from.

"Ah, shit," Mike says. "They were in a huff because Carl thought we sucked tonight." He stretches painfully and closes his eyes. "There's an artist about Katrina, believe it or not." He mumbles something, maybe, "Like you," but when I look to him to confirm this, he looks asleep.

Back at his apartment, Mike falls face-first onto the couch.

"I can feel every goddamn hole that's been put into me," he says.

I go into the kitchen and fetch an ice pack. "I never heard a crowd gag like that," I say. On my way back to the living room, I grab peroxide and a wad of cotton.

"That was disappointment," Mike says into the cushion. "Last time they saw us both fall onto razor wire, but that shit cut me up so bad I couldn't shower for a week."

I sit on the edge next to him and rub the ice pack gently over the red bumps in his shoulder. I know it's bullshit, but I keep telling myself this is *not* what Katrina will be doing for Carl. I have a lighter touch, since I have such sensitive hands. After chilling the thumbtack wounds, I put the ice on the back of Mike's neck and grab the peroxide, just like Mike says to do.

The thumbtack wounds look ready to infect, despite the peroxide. After a rubdown all over his back, Mike sits up. He has me get behind him, then leans back until I must be lost from view. He is pressed so hard against me I can feel his groans in my breasts.

"Tell me what the hell I do this for again," he says as I rub his shoulders.

"You like the pay," I say.

Mike turns his head part of the way toward me. "I get paid?"

"And you get to meet exciting new people and count their teeth on one hand."

Mike laughs, then warns me not to make him laugh. "You should talk," he says. "You come to a wrestling match dressed like a math professor."

I give his shoulders a hard squeeze, though I'm sure he barely feels it. "Don't cross me," I say. "I got my own bag of thumbtacks."

"That'll have to wait for tomorrow night," he says. He closes his eyes and puts his head back. He has ridges on his forehead from the scars piled upon scars piled upon scars. He dozes a while, but when I start feeling claustrophobic I wake him. Then we clean the cut on his forehead, and he checks his back in the bathroom mirror.

"I'm going to look like Quasi fucking Moto," he says.

I show him how some rouge on his left shoulder evens out the thumbtack marks and gives his back a ruddy, healthy glow. He submits to this willingly with no hint of sarcasm, no sense that he's humoring me. He already knows how to apply some base to his forehead so his ridges are noticeable only from close-up. From five feet away, his body is smooth and healthy. He has me stand back to make sure of this.

Soon after that, we go to bed. As he's nodding off, Mike tells me three times that he needs to be touching me every moment while he's asleep. It sounds so important to him that I feel dishonest and undependable the one time I do slide out to check my messages.

The next night, it's like this:

We're naked, and Mike breaks out body paint, the heavy duty Ultimate Warrior stuff that goes on thick and rubs off only with a hard sweat. We paint targets on each other's bodies. He paints KICK ME in cartoonish letters across my ass. When he turns off everything but the black light in his bedroom, we glow like aliens.

Then we go to the interview.

"Tonight," I say, "you have a big match with Pussy Galore" (the glint in his eyes, fury at the very mention of my wrestling name—his nemesis, his new greatest opponent). "What are your thoughts concerning your upcoming bout, this First Blood match, with this most fearsome adversary?"

"Pussy Galore," he screams, his beautiful naked body painted and glowing in the black light, an arrow and THE BUCK STOPS HERE hovering over his manly penis, which swells subtly as he goes into his act. "The things I'm going to do to that Pussy, so bad its own mother won't recognize it!" And here it's about breaking bones and bending bodies in unnatural ways, all of which he pantomimes with trained clarity.

No surprise that my messages last night were all from Martha. "Just checking up on you," she started with each time. By the third message her speech was groggy and slurred, her voice barely audible over the television.

"It'll help me rest," she finally admitted in the last one, "if I know you're home safe, so give a ring whatever time you get in." She paused as though making sure there was only silence on the other end. Then, "I've got a dog story for you." Code —call me when *he's* not around.

I realize now, while Mike glows and struts and gesticulates violently before me, that I pity Martha for wanting to live in a sealed bubble of safety, and for me pity is the same as anger. I erased her messages and went back to bed. By the time Mike found me in the dark and pulled me up against him, I had decided that letting Martha worry about me for a day or two might teach her that there will always be things beyond her control.

I sidle backwards on the bed, lowering and lowering my guard to Mike, opening my painted body. I could taunt him, fuel him on some more, but there is a line you don't cross. Mike and I, our play puts our bodies so close to that line we can kiss it.

THE CAT STORY

An old woman shows up at my door to tell me my cat is dead. This after I've spent all morning and a good part of the afternoon getting ready to hang myself. The old woman is at least seventy, nearly toothless, disheveled. She carries a paper sack, the bottom rounded at the edges like a curling puck.

"It was a Buick who did it," she says. She thumbs over her shoulder toward the street, where there is no Buick. No aura of recent death, no hint of an accident. I don't know why I'm even looking. I don't have a cat. My gaze strays to the neighbors' lawns—manicured, sculpted, uniform. The kind of neighborhood that will shudder with disgust at a local hanging.

"A Buick?" I say. "How do you know it's my cat?"

"Your cat," she says. She scratches her scalp through her shower cap. "Got hit in front of your house."

If she has the cat in that sack, it's balled up pretty tight. The mouth of the sack is worn in her grip.

"Who sent you?" I haven't ventured to open the door wider than the width of my face. This isn't even my house— it's my grandmother Peg's—but she's in Florida for the season and I'm supposed to be getting my life back together. Obviously, Peg's offer hasn't done much good.

"I got nothing to do with nothing," the old woman says.

"Thought I was doing a favor. You can just bury it out back you know." Artfully, she looks around and above me, avoiding my eyes with precise near-misses.

How long has she walked around with that cat? She must have walked for days from the looks of her. Her quilted housecoat has grass and mud stains that make its true color hard to discern. "What if I told you I didn't have a cat?"

"Liar," she says, still scratching her head.

"Maybe it's best you came in." I'm already quite an item of gossip in this neighborhood, the equivalent of an idiot-manchild locked away in the root cellar. Now, Peg's poor excuse of a grandson, who's given up stability and marriage for artistic endeavor, is making things worse by humoring a dirty homeless woman on the front stoop. I can feel the neighbors watching us, their property values sinking into their lower intestines. I open the door all the way.

Her slippered feet slap against the tile floor. She keeps a gentle hand under the bottom of the sack, reinforcing it but reverential about not poking its contents.

I hesitate from offering her a seat. There's the kitchen chair I brought out so I could do my business with the light fixture, but it's in exactly the right spot and I don't want to go through all that rigmarole again. This being my grandmother Peg's house, the sofa, loveseat and armchair are all covered in plastic, but still I worry that the old woman's grime will seep through. Bad enough I plan to leave behind a swinging body to clean up, but also the stink of a filthy old lunatic and her dead cat? I motion toward the kitchen chair. "Sit?"

The old woman sits with determination and plops the sack onto her lap. More of a thud. The sack has some serious weight to it.

I take my seat on the sofa, directly across from her so there we are, face to face, the coffee table and my rejected book between us like a wall built far too low. I reach for my glass of gin but think better of it. I have no intention of offering her any. The generic rejection letter clipped to my book reads, "Dear Writer." I haven't read the rest; with an opening like that, why bother? I doodled next to their salutation so it now reads, "Dear Writer-my-ass."

The old woman sits up as though ready to withstand police interrogation. She has every intention of protecting the sack in her lap.

"Coke?" she says abruptly. "Coke? You got Coke here?"

"It's all warm," I lie. "It's sitting in a cupboard."

"A little ice will do the trick. I can help you dig that hole if you give me a Coke."

I sink deeply into the sofa, the kind of sofa that's a struggle to get up from again. To the right of my book sits my phone. Three new messages—all from my wife, one every other day for the past week, each one no doubt prompted by grandmother Peg, a new effort to pull me out of my hole. I watched each one pop up on the screen after the electronic bloop. The first one said, Hello Brad, it's Marsha. Then, Hope you're doing better. Been thinking of you. The most recent, Call me if you want. Grandmother Peg no doubt floated some promise of inheritance if Marsha took me back. I haven't found any reason to respond.

I'm not the type anyone would have ever taken for a writer, including me—a stable though generally unaffectionate marriage, a well-off and aging grandmother, and a steady job as Associate Manager of Space for a 40-story office building, my prime responsibility chair inventory and allocation. I was going over inventory sheets in my office one day, and I suddenly wanted to have Charlie Rose interview me about my novel. I thought what an interesting story my sudden, unprompted calling would make to start off the interview.

I brought home a dozen legal pads that night and stacked them on the piano in the den. All through dinner, as Marsha fished for compliments on her brown rice with wakami, I wrote questions Charlie Rose might ask me so I would have some natural-sounding, thoughtful responses: How do you know you weren't just struck by a sudden bout of midlife crisis? and Talk about how the position of Associate Manager of Space prepared you to be such a methodical and assertive novelist. After dinner I went straight to the den and made a start. The going was tough, since I had to make things up from scratch. After she finished loading the dishes, Marsha came into the den with an exotic food catalog. She sat on the edge of the recliner as though in a doctor's waiting room and opened the catalog, but she didn't read a thing.

"How long does a novel take?" she asked, her pretty brown eyes trying their best to understand something about what I was doing.

"I write for a while," I said, stooped over the cover of the piano keys, "and then it will be finished." I didn't have much yet—a description of some weather, and a guy coming home from work. Marsha said, "Hmm," as though she understood perfectly, and went back to her catalog. The turning of pages sounded like jelly slapped through a ventilation grate.

"It can't be all that long," she said. Marsha didn't read novels. Magazines were practical and functional, catalogs an utter necessity, though she would sometimes admire the layout of the cover a Clive Cussler or a John Grisham I was reading. "I mean, if it took all that long, it wouldn't be worth all that bother, would it?" As she spoke, I could feel my brain numbing, acupuncture on the hypothalamus.

"You need to leave me alone," I said. Marsha looked at me as if I had just told her she had a cancerous bulb on her cheek. "You need to get out and leave me alone," I said. Funny—not once had I asked Charlie Rose to give me a moment to thank my patient and understanding wife.

Marsha closed the catalog and held it to her chest as she left.

As I wrote, it was all think and drink, think and drink, write a little, then back to the thinking and the drinking. I went right to it every day after work, all morning and afternoon on my days off. In the evenings I slept off the heavy drunk I accumulated during the day. Marsha checked up on me every now and then. I could smell hope, like moldy water, swell up in her when she'd find me slumped uncomfortably in the leather recliner or reading the label on a bottle of Wild Turkey, my messy pages scattered around the piano.

"I'm making dinner," she'd say for instance, her voice tinged with a hint of warning, of her need for things to be normal again. "Do you want me to put lemon in the curry?" Maybe she counted on me to announce failure so she could comfort me briefly and pack me an alfalfa salad for lunch the next day, our life back to brief kisses and semi-annual intimacy. I ignored her the best I could, feeling with her every intrusion a desire to throw pencils at her ankles.

So I wrote at the office, chair requests and locations ignored or handled sloppily to let me focus on my real work. The office building fell into chaos, unclaimed task chairs stranded in hallways, mail sorters sorting in leather executive high-backs. Marsha hid my manuscript pages, so I put her silk blouses in the dryer on high. She said, "Oh, great," every time she saw me with a pen. I slept in the living room and promised things would be back to normal when I finished. It took three months of note pads and pens and pencils and bottles of liquor that fueled my creative fire, and getting fired to boot, but I finished my novel. I told Marsha our troubles would be over when I typed it up and got it published. She did her best to pretend I didn't live in the house anymore while I researched agents and book publishers. As I sent my novel out, I imagined the letter of acceptance, rife with compliments. I planned my book tour, practiced my mannerisms, invented witticisms to sign my name under. Late at night, I could hear Marsha crying on the phone. I imagined literate groupies, bodies tingling in my presence. With each rejection, I moved my book from one envelope to the next, sure that this time someone would see the light.

My grandmother Peg lent me her house when Marsha finally asked me to leave. Marsha never asked me directly, to tell the truth. She told grandmother Peg, and grandmother Peg told me. Marsha wouldn't make any effort to talk to me except to pull open the zippers on my best pants. In retaliation, I sawed into the straps of her bras with a nail file so they would break while she was wearing them.

Grandmother Peg's offer was not one of kindness. It was

to get this 'writing thing' out of me, to let it run its course like a stomach virus. She sent me the keys express mail. That night, she called from her larger house in Florida.

"The summer house is yours," she said. "Send your book to every name you can find. See how no one wants it and for God's sake go back to Marsha."

"And also for God's sake, Brad," she added. She paused to let her next statement sink in. "Brad. Brad. Dry out and give up and go back to your life." This was four months ago, and she told me she was going to need the house again in four and a half.

None of this sounds like good justification for a hanging, but I've given up on finding a good reason. I spent most of the morning making sure the chair was in the right place so I could stand on it comfortably with the belt around my neck and kick the chair away easily to give me no way of backing out. Then I started doing dry runs, swinging by my arms to make sure the light fixture would hold me up long enough to kill me, each run separated by an hour on the couch, where I drank and got my courage up for another go. It's one thing to practice your death, another to get off the couch to practice it again. Just before the old woman came knocking, I was wondering if I was up for a dress rehearsal.

"About this cat," I say to the old woman.

"Your cat," she says defensively, "out in the road nothing I could do about that. Just sitting there doing what cats do in the middle of the road acting like nothing's going to happen to him safe as all shit and suddenly there's this car this Mazda this brown shoebox thing."

"A Buick?" I say.

"Yes a Buick I said Buick no way you can prove otherwise." The woman scootches up a little, her housecoat crackling. "This here Buick isn't from around here it was obvious speeding down the road in a neighborhood like this a nice neighborhood like this one speeding down the road like that the cat had it coming. You can bury it under a tree in some shade."

I'm ready for her to pull the cat out of her sack by the hind legs and lay it out on the coffee table like a butcher displaying a plucked chicken. I move my rejected book aside. I notice how much "Writer-my-ass" stands out, along with my doodles around the clean, mock-literary typeface of the company letterhead. The font that suggests serenity and insight. The doodles are of hanged stick figures. I can't remember how many times my book has been rejected now, but it seems to come back more quickly every time I send it out. I slide the rejection note from under the paper clip and gradually turn it over.

Meanwhile, the old woman is still at it: "And if you think I blame that Buick that Chevy any you think wrong. But boy was it coming down the road coming down quick cuz he couldn't have known what kind of neighborhood it was not being from around here and Friskie got it all in one shot at least just got run over and shut his eyes and that was that."

"Friskie?" I pet the rejection slip until it's flat.

"You named him," she says. She points to make sure I know who thought up that stupid name. "All those cats how are you going to find an original name for all of them? He likes Friskies so you call him Friskie. The black and white you call Oreo what else? Sylvester the other black and white. Mittens Cracker Big Balls you can't go not giving them names you know." She looks sentimental and a little misty-eyed talking about my cats.

"How many cats in all?"

She slumps as though strategic wires have been cut. A look of futility. "Your damn cat mister," she says.

The sun is coming down. The shades at the old woman's back glow appropriately. I have one hand on my rejected book; I am considering whether to leave it behind or destroy it before I go.

The book I've written is this:

A futures analyst, Phil, depressed and stuck in his job, quits and runs off to Mexico, where he beds Latina identical twins and tries his hand at bounty hunting after a chance meeting with a one-eyed midget who gives him cryptic advice about life over a session of tequila. Phil finds he has a knack for this kind of work, and on his first time out he brings to justice the head of a notorious drug cartel and steals a briefcase full of drug money that befriended DEA agents discover but let him drive off with in a scene of touching camaraderie. Phil returns home, determined to resume his life now that he's sown his wild oats. But the suburban lifestyle leaves him wanting, and after a well honed and witty speech to his patient but unsympathetic wife, something like the end of *A Doll's House* with muscle, he goes off into the night, his future uncertain but chock full of potential for gunplay.

The old woman suddenly pulls a faded pea green scarf from the pocket of her housecoat.

"I make these myself," she says, the silk scarf crumpled in her hand, a far cry from any kind of lucrative presentation. "You got four dollars? I could use four dollars right now. Four dollars and a ride."

It's not what she says or how she says it, but something about the old woman inspires the perfect idea in me.

"I write," I tell her.

She glances sidelong at me, the first time our eyes have met. She rubs her cheek with the scarf, and she clutches the paper sack a little tighter, as though I've just told her I'm a rapist of old women. "You make money with that?"

"I just write," I tell her.

"Not buying no damn story," she says. "And I'm not taking one for this scarf. Don't need that shit. Don't need to be carrying around no story I got nothing to do with," she says.

"But you do," I tell her.

Again, the brief meeting of the eyes. If we go on like this, we'll be married by nightfall.

"You drunk?" she says. "All I need is a dollar."

"It's a story about cats," I tell her. "Cats and scarves and grandmothers who wrap everything they own in plastic. It's got all the reasons why you can't go home anymore. It's about being down to dill pickles in the fridge, about the last days of the siege. Coke with no ice and the wives who leave their men because their men like Coke that way. It's about the clarity that happens sometimes right before the end." All this comes together in me like particles orbiting a gravity well, collapsing into the inevitable brilliance of a new star.

"That's a weird story," she says.

"I'll send you a copy."

"Don't read no damn stories." She lifts the sack to her chest and stands. "Don't got no goddamn stories cuz I don't need no goddamn stories and they got nothing to do with me I ain't in no goddamn goddamn story." She makes for the door. "Fucking stories no ice this house smells like pork like a fucking pig." Before she leaves, she pauses a moment in the doorway. "Great stinking pig is how it smells I won't give my tits to know how you keep your pecker up in here!"

I sit up. The couch creaks like couches in a grandmother's house do. I hear the old woman still yelling out about my pecker and all as she rumbles down the street.

It's a beautiful ending—the perfect idea that doesn't get written, its only living vestiges rolling in pieces around the head of an old woman trying to find her kitty's final resting place. I rise and take my novel out back to toss it. I'll leave nothing behind but a half bottle of gin, some Cuervo and a little apricot brandy. Let them admire nothing but the strength of the knot in my belt, how I chose the stem of the light fixture rather than the paltry branches to swing from. An artist's death. Grandmother Peg will shudder in disappointment at the thought of me. Marsha won't be able to contain her anger. I am past needing affirmation for my work. I feel more ready now than I have all day.

Out back, I pause over the trashcan. I consider digging a hole in the yard, but some birds nearby distract me. They're small, brown birds, I don't know what kind. Quick and electric in movement, but deceptively preoccupied. They seem too easy and inviting to reach out, grab and crush. My manuscript lands with a loud slap on top of yesterday's trash, and I go back inside.

DOGS

Nels: He's got a bad case of dogs. I'm over there, at his place, at least once a week when it gets hot like this, and it's worse than mine. He talks sometimes like he's going to buy a tank of cyanide gas and flood his holes with it, but I know that it's never going to happen. It's not just because you can't see how much damage you done; got to do with the black-footed ferrets. The sheriff wouldn't let me or Nels take a leak in private if he knew we had us some cyanide. The ferrets are dropping all over, dying of rabies.

It's tough believing they're out there, dug deep in the colonies, feeding on dogs late at night. I don't know how they stand it; imagine being surrounded by what you feed off. It's rare if they ever come out during the day for any reason. Matter of fact, I've never seen them. Cyanide hits the ferrets the worst, but we'll never be rid of dogs. I don't know what took me so long to figure it out. I used to think we could do them in.

The only part I don't like is the sitting and waiting, waiting for a dog to take the bait. I don't remember anymore who showed who the best way to do this. We did other things, me and Nels. That's years back, but I remember. You leave bits of onion stems just outside their holes, and parsley leaves, and they fall for it every time. Nailing a dog anywhere with a

30-30'll pretty much finish it off, unless you go blasting off a foot, but that might even do the trick. All you need see is that spray or chunk of blood and fur to tell you it's done for. I seen some practically split in half. Dogs don't quiver or lie there kicking when they die. Either they're up and scurrying about, or they're stone dead. Even when they can get themselves back up and in their holes, it don't matter. There's always more coming. Nels is pretty good at getting heads. We drink as we wait. It's something to do.

Nels and me shared a woman once. She was a nurse. She wore white shoes, and Nels and me almost went ahead and killed each other over her, but I'm not holding anything against Nels. Never bothered finding out what's become of her. Not that it matters. I never ask Nels if he's forgotten because I don't have to. He's still coming over. You sit with your feet up on the rail, barrel fixed between your heels, stock on your lap. We like to keep our ammo boxes on the armrests right behind our beers so we can reload quickly.

Baiting always works. The dogs keep coming.

Nels pegs another. It gets its whole head spread out over its back like a sweatshirt hood and drops flat. It's keeping clear out today; the sun's high against the field. It makes dog flesh a deep, dark red and look really juicy. Things only get clearer. When it's like this, I can almost believe that group who still says the world is flat. I don't believe I can see Cheyenne from here or nothing, but things do look level, like you just might be able to see some things if you looked hard enough. Nels used to grin over his headshots. He'd even toast himself: raise his beer and tip it. Now they're just a fact of life.

"Little shit," he says, resting the barrel in the V he makes with his boots. You have to keep your feet up high on the porch rail so the barrel don't touch your legs. A barrel gets hot on a day like this. My dog-shooting boots have dents softened in the arches. "Give it up," he says, picking up his beer, keeping his trigger-hand in place. Since Nels and me don't talk much anymore—not much reason to—he talks to himself sometimes. He wipes his face on the can, but he won't stop sweating. Not just because the beers are warm: he glistens on days like this. We never bother getting ice for the cooler.

I used to think it'd be easier if we each covered the half-field in front of us, but I can always see Nels in the corner of my eye when I'm scanning my half and I know he can keep his eye on me. Nels covers the right half. I got a feeling one's coming, so I put down my beer and put my hand on the grip of the barrel. I always keep my trigger-hand ready.

I think a lot how easy it'd be to shoot him: Nels. Just pick up my .30-.30 like I'm going after a dog, turn it on him and pull. I think about it most times I go to pick off a dog. I think about it the most when he's aiming himself. I used to wonder if he'd just shoot me back.

I have my chance again. A dog peeks out, sniffs, then comes out all the way. I aim, but I can see Nels moving in the corner of my eye and I miss. "Fuck," I say. I level off, and the dog freezes. They're that stupid. Like all dogs live for is to get shot. A miss like that makes you remember how far you're into the day. Nels was just drinking.

The second shot is on the mark: right through the gut. The dog runs back into its hole, floundering. It happens that way sometimes. You see the spray, then the dog takes off like you just stomped your foot, like all that got it was the sound of the gun firing. I used to think they blocked up the holes they ran back into, leaving fewer to cover, but it isn't long before dogs are coming out those same holes again. They crawl all over themselves to get shot.

I was on a bourbon drunk and pissed when I first wanted to kill Nels, and I burst in on him and that woman. Nels picked up this pipe and took such a bad swing at me that he fell, and I had a clear alley. He was lying there, drunk, buck-naked and looking stupid, and he probably would have died that way if I had had any guts. I probably could have even done him in with just my whittling knife. It wouldn't have taken much to put the blade in the soft spot of his throat and cut up, right through his Adam's apple, but no. I just stood there with my .38 cocked, listening to that woman scream, Stop! Stop it!

Nels and me were just fighting when he first had his chance. We'd do that now and then: fight. Sometimes we did it so we could get ourselves kicked out of bars, sometimes not, but that night we were going at it over that woman, and then Nels pulled out a 9mm and clicked off the safety. He would've had to plug me a few times since he was aiming at my gut, but I wanted him to go ahead and do me in. I dared him; I opened my shirt, as if I had a target painted on me, and I slapped myself on the belly and said to him, "Go ahead," and I meant it. Sometimes I'd get so mad I'd wish either one of us would go ahead and do the other.

A dog catches one through the side of the neck. It flinches at first, as if Nels had missed, but then it just stops and keels over, oozing. I keep wondering how much it takes dogs to realize they're bleeding. It's like the ones that run when they're done for: how much does it take to realize that you're dead? This one falls right next to the others Nels has put away from the same hole. We call those the 'meat holes' because they're like meat grinders. Dogs get squeezed out, and then they fall flat, leaving red stains and wet chunks of flesh all over. I can usually keep an exact dog-count when we first start out, but when we're getting on in the day, I can only be sure we're running about average. The first ones we shot today are already starting to steam. When the afternoon surge starts slowing down like this, the field looks like a war zone. It looks bad for dogs, but their strength is in their endless numbers.

Nels pulls his Browning into his lap and puts his feet down so he can reload. He does it quickly, but dogs never appear when you're reloading. It's like the sound of empty cases hitting the porch floor makes them nervous. It's not that I don't trust Nels, but I always reload quickly, like I'm just getting ready for another dog.

Nels loses a lot of aim the more he drinks. Every now and then, when he's at that point, he looks like he's about to take off his toes, but it's like something won't let him. It makes him pull up in the nick of time. Maybe it's his rifle; it's a Browning and it's got kickback. The blades of the rocker he sits in have worn grooves into the porch. He's done the same to the porch at his house.

We're running low now. The dogs are starting to lose interest, as if they know when we've had enough. I used to think we were rid of dogs at the end of an afternoon, even when I'd see more the next day, but one time, right after Nels left, I went out and felt the field bulging with dogs. I was sure I could even hear it: piles of dog-sex going on right under my feet.

I still didn't learn my lesson right then and there. Not completely; first I got stupid and started thinking maybe dogs have some sort of order, where me and Nels get rid of the useless part of the herd, or clan, or whatever you call a bunch of dogs, like me and Nels were dog-gods, wiping out misfits. The smart dogs coax the dumb dogs out of the holes, and the dog-gods strike them down. I don't think that anymore. I know better now.

Nels picks up his Browning for one more, and I already know it's the last one of the afternoon. Nels says, "Last one," because he knows it too, and he pegs it through the chest. He couldn't do a headshot at the end of an afternoon if his life depended on it.

Not even then.

We don't clean up the field because Packer-down-the-road's Dobermans will feed on the carcasses during the night, or whatever ferrets might be left, and what they don't eat is usually taken off by the carrion birds or cleaned off by bugs. I used to wonder if more dogs were disappearing than there were ways for them to go—as if dogs could bring in their own dead—but there's no smarts to dogs. That's what I know now. They breed, then peek out of a hole after some bait, then get plugged, then get chomped on by whatever feels like a little dog meat. That's all there is to it.

Nels puts his feet down, holding his Browning away from him so the barrel don't touch his legs, and gets up. He holds the rifle by the trigger-guard, pointed at the floor, to unload. He usually don't start popping bullets until I'm about to.

We don't say good-bye anymore. I don't see much sense to it. I know when I'm supposed to be at his place so we can work on his dogs. He goes around the side of the house and has to make a long walk down the trail to get to his truck. He used to walk backward, making good-byes and yelling jokes the whole way, but he walks with his back to me now.

I like to stand out in the field and aim at him. The ammo boxes are always back on the porch, but I'm in the habit of keeping a couple of shells handy. I don't remember anymore if I started doing this after I felt him aiming at my back while I was leaving his place, or if I started this myself. If you pump your target in the spine, it'll just fall and lie there, paralyzed. It probably won't die right away, but you're open to plug it a couple more times until it's finished. If you put your shot between the backbone and the shoulder blade, you'll probably puncture a lung, which'll kill your target eventually, and it'll still be able to get back at you before it kicks it. It's a tricky spot to get at, but Nels walks slowly and steadily, so I'd have little trouble. There's just this one thick muscle guarding the back of the lung. A well-placed bullet'll slice through it like tissue paper, and Nels always wears a T-shirt that really shows it off. He'll probably feel himself dying, then spin around, going into his pocket, for his chance.

THE WOMAN AND THE DOG

Sometimes I just sit here, making up things.

I have a company, "Writer, Ink."

I don't write until I got the sell: fantasy, mystery, etc. Fantasy mag wants a story with a unicorn, I write a story with a unicorn. Mystery rag: two bodies on a train? Two bodies on a train. Ditto for porn.

The money is porn.

I write forum letters. No real readers write those letters—at least, they're not writing letters worth publishing. Sex in a glass elevator? No problem. Threesomes? Foursomes? Piece of cake. Midgets? Yup, we got midgets. My agent gives me the pitch, I put it together, soon comes the check.

Cushy.

Other times—most times, honestly—I'm on the couch in my robe, waiting on a pitch. I watch talkies and game shows, then the soaps, and on into the news. While my girlfriend is at work, I sit with Matilda under my arm.

Matilda is our dog. She's part pit bull, part other things.

Mostly pit bull.

Sometimes, Matilda chews on her rawhide while sitting with me.

Sometimes, Matilda watches the talkies.

Sometimes, I let her watch *Sesame Street.*

My girlfriend waits tables at T.G.I. Friday's.

A shame, really, because she studied psychology and she's good at it. For instance:

She's good at dropping hints about commitment. Every now and then, she'll tell me out of the blue how long we've been living together, how many months now. She never counts in years—she always opts for the bigger number.

"You know we've lived together twenty-six months?" she'll say.

She would probably count it in weeks, even days, if she took the time to do the math.

Also, she calls Matilda our 'baby.' I'm Daddy, she's Mummy. Sometimes, she makes like Matilda can talk.

"Can we go out now, Daddy?" she'll say, a childish lilt to her voice, when Matilda is standing by the back door. Or, "I've been a good girl, haven't I, Daddy?" when Matilda stands expectantly by the cupboard where we keep her dried pig ears and rawhide bones. "Don't good girls get treats?"

Or, when Matilda is licking my face after my girlfriend kisses me: "It's okay, Daddy, let me get Mummy's smell off you."

My girlfriend probably thinks me dense for not getting her hints. She's got a good case for it: only now do I realize just how many she drops.

All this, and the only work she can find right now is Friday's. I'd be humiliated. She has to wear all kinds of buttons on her work apron. Stupid buttons. Buttons with stupid things on them.

Check these out:

SMILE PATROL

WHY BE NORMAL?

BIBO ERGO SUM: I DRINK, THEREFORE I AM

See?

When she first got the job, they grilled her until she could recite the desserts and sing their birthday song at a moment's notice. Sometimes, she hums the song without knowing it. Then I do, also without knowing it. Then she yells at me, "Stop," as if I'm teasing her.

Then, my agent calls with a new pitch: 'a woman and a dog.' My girlfriend, smelling of burger grease and smoke, figures I'm already doing the research (that is, research on zoophilia), might as well get paid for the effort.

My girlfriend thinks I'm fooling around with the dog.

My retort: "Hey, they want a *woman* and a dog."

Doesn't faze her.

Matilda sticks her face between ours, her tongue forcing its way between our lips, when me and my girlfriend kiss. If I give my girlfriend a kiss first when she comes home from work, the dog won't touch her face. If it's my girlfriend who kisses me first, Matilda launches on my face, licking all over.

My girlfriend says it's proof. I got plenty of opportunity...that's her other proof. I'm around all day, so's the dog, and with my girlfriend out working, what's to stop us?

With my girlfriend, it's all cause and effect—the clear, rational and empirical breakdown of events in linear time, the effect being this aforementioned attraction the dog has for her daddy, the cause either nature (Elektra complex) or nurture (me).

Also:

My girlfriend says Matilda licks mostly the spot she just kissed.

I can't tell. All I know is, I got dog slobber everywhere: my glasses slimed, my beard sticky.

"I think the dog's too old for this kind of complex to be natural," she'll conclude.

The dog is twenty-four months old.

So this is how I figure the woman and the dog story:

She comes home, and the dog is all into the flour and the sugar and the cherry syrup. The dog is a bulldog with a penis like a lipstick tube, she's seen it. He's strong and protective of her, always checking out her latest man. Rarely approving. She's always felt that the dog is looking out for her best interests, so when he doesn't approve, she doesn't put out. Hence, she's gone without for months.

Remember this—this is important.

The dog is all dirty and sticky and syrupy. (Cherry syrup is a big thing in porn—for your average porn reader, cherry syrup let loose upon something, anything, male, female, animal or mineral, is almost guaranteed arousal.) She takes him upstairs and gives him a bath. She feels slight arousal at running her hands over his strong shoulders, burly chest and strong, wiry legs. His long, red penis appears, though it is not hard. Still, she notices. What a man this would be, she thinks...but no, she can't, this is a dog after all.

Suspense for the reader: she wants to, she wants to, but she's not giving in yet. This is porn, after all, so what the readers expect is men wanting to, girls wanting to, hot and ready no matter what they say, so why delay it much?

Bait.

Everyone knows it's going to happen, so what good porn does is delay it, keeps your average porn customer baited, waiting, the erection at half-mast, ready for the big plunge. That's why you have long stints of a guy walking up the stairs, checking his shirt, smoothing his mustache in all the better movies, or a couple in bed, talking about nothing in particular (actor improvisation, I'll bet) when you know you'd rather see them doing something else.

But, you can't hold it off too long...

She can't believe it! This canine penis mesmerizes her—so manly it is, so energetic. It would give her so much more than what she's not been getting, she is sure.

And, as if he knows what she's thinking, the dog suddenly thrashes around in the water, drenching her to the skin, and she goes to her room, takes off her clothes, is about to put on a bathrobe, when...

She's aroused. Damn it to hell, but she is, and she knows what she wants and it doesn't matter anymore if she's not supposed to have it. She takes the peanut butter jar on the table by her bed (I'll explain earlier that she likes to snack on peanut butter before going to sleep) and starts coating herself with it, an area sensitive to her touch right now, excitable.

Here's the lead in:

"I can't believe I'm doing this, but yet I can, and somehow I can't believe I never did this before, because it seems so easy to me now, such an easy way to have what I really want, and I start back towards the bathroom, walking with my legs apart so the peanut butter will remain thickly coated over my hot, anxious, pulsating passion, and I call out, 'Skippy, come get your peanut butter...'"

My girlfriend has a few problems with my story. The main thing is that the peanut butter idea is stolen. Worse, it's stolen from her, kind of.

Before Friday's, my girlfriend worked for the city courts, typing up transcripts. Once she transcribed a case where a newlywed husband and his family decided to throw a surprise party for his wife. They all hid in the basement with the lights off and took the dog as bait. Surely, she'd come looking for the dog down there, and the party would be sprung.

So the wife comes home. They get the dog to bark a couple times. The wife makes some commotion, then comes down into the basement.

"Fido" (or Spot, or whatever, I forget), she says, "come get your peanut butter."

Then the lights fly on.

She skipped town that night. The case was a divorce hearing in absentia—no one had heard from her in months. To this day, as far as I know.

My girlfriend has trouble believing things happened that way. She thinks this is just a story the husband and his folks concocted to cover up something rather nasty.

Who knows, she'll muse sometimes, maybe even something sinister.

What don't let her buy it are the following:

1). Why would the party have only the husband and his relatives? None of her friends? Her own family? What kind of a party is that?

2). If the woman came home and heard the dog barking in the basement, she would probably think something's wrong, and far be it from any woman to get naked and spread peanut butter on herself when there might be danger in the house.

3). Besides, my girlfriend will add, if they were in the basement and she was at the top of the stairs (she couldn't have gotten much past the first stair without noticing all these people in her basement), there's no way they could have noticed peanut butter between her legs before she retreated.

"On her breasts, maybe," she'll add to that.

Funniest thing, though—in all her logical arguments against the likeliness of such an occurrence, she never once dismissed it all in her knowledgeable, studied demeanor with a: "Besides, no woman would ever go and *do* a thing like that."

What really bothers her, I gather, is that she suspects that I use us to write porn quite often.

Even when I write love scenes for fantasy mags (often involving beautiful, seductive elfin women or dryads or passionate, desperate love right before a hopeless battle with Orcs), to me it's me and my girlfriend there. Granted, the names are changed and the acts exaggerated, so it might not be all that obvious, but in my mind, there's me and her, swapping with another couple after a party that's gone a bit too far, or unbuckling our scabbards to reach unhinderedly at our quivering, excited flesh, etc. It's so obvious to me, I get nervous when she goes reading my stuff.

Most of the time, though, she doesn't seem to make the connection. That, or she thinks my sex scenes are all being acted out with other women.

Then again, maybe she does put it all together; she's pretty smart, after all. Maybe what she's trying to figure out is which came first. When we try something new in our relationship, is it because we are inspired on our own, and then I write about it, or is the reverse true?

To tell the truth, I don't have an answer.

All I know is the woman and the dog story was a hit, and now I've got more offers—some dog, others others. One's even for a scene with a bull: how cruel, how mythological.

MRS. BOYLAN, WIDOWED

Mrs. Boylan next door put up a new clothesline. The old one had fallen months ago—this was back in mid-February, in the midst of a deep cold. The line froze through and broke like licorice sticks, three pieces. A shirt fell with it, too, one of Mrs. Boylan's blouses. The bottom hem stuck in the ground and the whole frozen garment stood there, dead still dead still, frozen as a February afternoon.

It was fine with me and Hazel that Mrs. Boylan would no longer be hanging her wash on her front porch for all to inspect. But one of her hanging poles was gone too (actually just lying useless in the back yard after being uprooted, maybe, by some kids in March), and one side of her new line was now strung from my hanging pole.

My wife didn't agree with this, either.

"You talk to her," she told me, the both of us studying from our dining room the infiltrating inches of line as if waiting for it to do something further. "You offer to put back up her pole, if that's what it takes."

My wife, Hazel, has little stomach for a fight.

Mrs. Boylan answered in a robe.

"You were about to take a bath?" I asked, intruding.

"No," she said.

"I won't keep you."

It was getting dark. I went to the kitchen, the back door, switched on the light in the back. "There," I said, pointing to my side of the new line.

"It was the Samson boy," Mrs. Boylan said.

"He should have put up your pole," I said.

"He was in a rush. I thought he would."

"You need to give clearer instructions."

Mrs. Boylan went back to the living room. I turned to one of the kitchen windows and shrugged for the benefit of my wife, though I couldn't see her out there, next door now, and followed Mrs. Boylan into the living room.

Mrs. Boylan was sitting back on the sofa. All the shades were to. Somehow, I hadn't noticed this before. Mrs. Boylan had her robe open, her slip and panties extended all out of shape.

I looked again. All the shades were to. No light in the room, so no shadows. I didn't think too much about it. Hazel would be watching for some sign of progress, so it had to be quick. I went over to Mrs. Boylan. I don't find women my age much attractive, but still. We did what we did. Afterwards, I went back home.

"And?"

"It was the Samson boy," I said. "He did it."

"Of course." Hazel nodded and considered the matter closed.

I started stealing trashcans.

It began on a sleepless night, just two nights after the thing with Mrs. Boylan. I had no worries about Hazel. I was awake with the impulsiveness of the whole episode, as though Mrs. Boylan and I had done this before. I was awake with how quickly it all happened, how quickly it was over. She zipped me up nice as you please and told me, "I'm sorry for any trouble, Mr. Burns." The next day I put up her fallen pole and rehitched her line. I gave it a good, tight knot, a sheepshank. Mrs. Boylan thanked me and wished me good day and had me walk around the outside of her house.

That sleepless night I was also wondering if the Samson boy got the same for his services. Certainly, there was no talk around the neighborhood that Mrs. Boylan was like that.

So there I was, wide-awake, and I heard the garbage truck make its run. I heard the hollow thumps of freshly empty Rubbermaids making their way down the street.

I got up. Hazel stirred a little, I think, but I didn't think I was doing anything suspicious at the time and so worried little about disturbing her.

I put on a robe and slippers and went out. The lawn was damp and chilly, giving my heels impersonal licks as I trudged forward. The neighborhood was quiet, except for the fading sound of the garbage truck, the fading conversation of trashmen.

I took a hold of my lone garbage can and started rolling it back up the driveway. I paused a second and saw two cans in front of Mrs. Boylan's, their tops face up in the grass like unfortunate turtles. I went over and took one of her cans. I rolled both mine and the other to the side of the garage, then reconsidered. The other can had BOYLAN written on it in thick, black marker. Below, an address that was not mine but close. So I took the Boylan can back to my tool shed. Plenty of room. I went back to bed and lay there until Hazel woke. I pretended to sleep until she went downstairs to start the coffee. Then I went to the bedroom window and looked out at the curb.

Mrs. Boylan still had only one trashcan sitting out there. Being awake the whole night made my previous actions feel more like a dream than if I had actually dreamed them. The daylight seemed alien and harsh.

Later that morning, Mrs. Boylan called. Hazel answered, but I could tell.

I was finishing breakfast. Hazel leaned against the archway into the living room. Effectively blocking any escape I might have been planning.

"Yes," Hazel said when she realized who it was. "Yes. Yes." She nodded. "Did they? No. No, we got ours, didn't we?"

Now Hazel was looking to me. I was blowing on my coffee and nearly put the hot liquid straight to my lip. She swiveled the mouthpiece under her chin and she asked me, "Our trashcan was still there this morning?"

"What?" I asked. "What's that?" Somehow, I managed to return the cup to its saucer with hardly a drop spilled.

"Trashcan," Hazel said.

"I was up early and brought it in this morning. What of it?"

Hazel reassured Mrs. Boylan we had ours and left it at that. Once she hung up, she told me, "To think. As if we kept tabs on her trash. What would we want with a thing like a *trash*can?"

I hesitated to offer anything.

She came over and sat next to me. She smelled fiercely of baby powder that morning. "You saw her trashcans? Why were you up so early?"

I panicked. "The trash truck woke me," I said. "I was tired. I didn't even look around. Couldn't tell you if both of her cans were out there or not."

Hazel nodded as if all this solved it. "It would be just like that woman," she said. I did not press her for more.

Hazel never went to my tool shed and suspected nothing. Still, I almost pulled out the stolen can once to show her and confess, "It had nothing to do with what happened with Mrs. Boylan," though this would have begged its own explanation. I felt a confession would ease my mind, though the theft had nothing to do with Mrs. Boylan herself. I didn't think of her at all when I stole the trashcan. I never even identified the thing as Mrs. Boylan's during the whole process. It might as well have been Herb Stanfill's. Herb lived out behind my house.

So to prove it, I took one from across the street, from the Fieldings, the next week. Again, it was a sleepless night. This was never a habit of mine before on trash day.

I took from the Stahls, the McAffes, from old Dr. Rooter. One a week. These houses covered a good spread of the neighborhood. Going much farther from my own house made me nervous. The streetlights felt like roving beams casing the inside of a prison, but suspicion never seemed to turn to me.

The hardest part was lying there half the night, waiting for the revs and gasps of the municipal truck. Getting up was out of the question—it left the slightest opening for Hazel to finger me. The tool shed could hold at least ten more—despite the wheels, these cans stacked quite nicely.

We had Mrs. Boylan over for dinner one night. Hazel's idea, just to make it clear we had no hard feelings about the clothesline.

The women talked trashcans most of the evening. The Stanfills, the Stahls, the McAffes. Old Dr. Rooter, even.

"I've never heard so many complaints before," Hazel said.

"No, never," Mrs. Boylan agreed.

"Do you think they could just be getting lazy and throwing the cans in with the trash?"

"But why just one a week? It seems too regular." Mrs. Boylan quite studiously finished her peas. "More peas, please."

"Mr. McAffe called the city," Hazel said. I passed the peas. Hazel offered butter, which was turned down. "They took his name, but they didn't promise anything."

Mrs. Boylan spooned herself another helping. "For Christ's sake, are they eating the damn things?"

Hazel excused herself to check on the pie in the oven. The first couple of times Mrs. Boylan and I were left alone were tense for me, but since she showed no sign of knowing me beyond the general neighborhood affiliation, I stopped grasping for something to fill the silence between us.

While Hazel clinked through the silverware drawer, possibly for a fork to stick the pie with, Mrs. Boylan said, "You should be worried the most, with your one can and all. The way you stuff it, I'm surprised they haven't taken it just to teach you a lesson. Those people hate lifting much."

I shrugged. "Just been lucky, so far."

Mrs. Boylan hummed a kind of agreement. I looked at her for the slightest sign of avoidance, or secrecy, of hiding something for Hazel's sake, even just the recognition that she knew I was looking for something that she wasn't going to give me.

She just sat there, munching peas. I could tell by the way her jaw moved that she was smushing them on the roof of her mouth with her tongue. It made a nice, buttery paste—I had a habit of doing that, myself.

I started going to other neighborhoods, just to make sure my habit wasn't relegated to just my one little cluster of houses. I had to prowl around at first until I got down the sanitation department's schedule. I slept five hours a night tops and snapped awake at three a.m. without fail, even on weekends. I dreamed every now and then of trashmen being dragged behind me like beer cans behind newlyweds. "Move it along. Move it along," they yelled to me.

The cans were not so uniform in other neighborhoods. Besides, my tool shed was already full now—getting out the lawn mower was becoming dangerous business. So I started dumping cans soon after stealing them: in the park, in the river, at other addresses. I even went into the bad areas of town a couple times and had to steal while people were still out on the street, not even thinking of going to bed yet.

These were the easiest thefts, though they still made me nervous. I expected people to rush out after me after slamming the trunk closed on their emptied receptacles. I expected them to give chase, shout out, "I'm going to get you, mutherfucker, trash-can stealing mutherfucker," the works.

No one bothered. A woman watched me once. She was tall, even without her gargantuan high heels. She wore leopard-skin, tiger-skin, and a wig that would have frightened the color out of either of the two beasts.

"Hey," she called out, but it was the wrong kind of hey, far too familiar. "Hey, baby, you got a thing with trash or something?"

I hurried on my way.

At dinner, I smushed my peas, didn't complain about the lack of mustard in the frank and beans, did justice to Hazel's chicken. I routinely looked out the dining room windows, into the yard, to that shed. Mostly, it was just dark and I saw only a dark reflection of myself, but I would not have been surprised to see a signal fire, a bright flame stinking of scorched plastic.

"You look tense tonight," Hazel said between round-trips to the kitchen. "I don't think your early morning drives are doing you any good. Why don't you mow the yard tomorrow?"

I cut myself on a can my next time out. It was old and aluminum. The cut had a dark streak in it from the filthy, filthy, filthy can. The streak wouldn't come out even with a good washing. I washed so long, Hazel was up before I was done.

"Are you...not well, dear?" she said through the door. "Do you want me to start you some Alka-Seltzer?"

I played sick most of the morning. Hazel checked on me every half-hour. Mostly, she put her hand on my forehead and frowned at me sympathetically.

But she didn't complain any when I said I was going to mow the yard.

The stack of trashcans had tilted from neglect. If it started to fall, I wouldn't have had the strength to stop it. Crushed under the evidence of my crimes. I barely managed to get out the mower and slam the shed door. The stack struck up against it with a thwang.

Hazel had hung out sheets to dry. They made hallways of fabric I toted my way down and up. Every time I was in sight of the shed, I expected it toppled; every time I was in sight of Mrs. Boylan's back door, I expected to see her at it.

No such luck with either. I did the back yard, the sides, then on around to the front. I ran the mower back and forth over the same spots and watched Mrs. Boylan's windows. I waited for her shadow to head toward the front of her house. When it did, I pushed on over to her lawn. On my way, someone passed and honked. I nodded, my hands busy on the mower.

When I got over to Mrs. Boylan's lawn, she was watching me through a window. I waved with urgency, and she came out onto the front porch, cigarette in hand. Flowered dress, hair in a bun.

"Do your lawn?" I called out, my hand shading my eyes from the sun.

"Samson boy did it Thursday," she said. She scratched her nose with the hand that held the cigarette.

"It's warm," I said. "It's looking a little long already."

Mrs. Boylan took a cursory toke and said, while exhaling, "You'll get nothing for it."

I turned back. "Who needs it then?" I considered it a kind of victory. I left the mower against the shed.

The next morning I overslept: four-fifteen. In the dark, I went to the shed and opened it. I thought I'd see at least a silhouette of the stack as it fell, but I only heard the heavy thump. I pulled the trashcans out one at a time and heaved them over the fence into Mrs. Boylan's yard. The sound of them landing was louder than I expected, but no one seemed disturbed. I imagined how they'd look when the sun came up —like an explosion in a nearby Rubbermaid factory. Blue, cylindrical shrapnel. I left the bottom trashcan, Mrs. Boylan's, in my shed. I turned it upside down and made her address, written on the side in thick, black marker, look funny. At least, it would seem funny the next time I got to look at it.

THE TAFFY PULL

When Stanton came home a quarter past midnight, he still had on in his powder-blue work shirt and Eckerd's nametag. He hung his flannel on the wall rack in a careful effort to look sober.

"Stan," Joan called in a neutral tone from the easy chair. *M*A*S*H* was on the television, but she had no idea what episode. The nauseating, sweet smell of Wild Turkey mixed with Stan's cologne always put Joan on edge, but she didn't consider him dangerous tonight.

"The kids asleep?" Stanton asked, slowly.

"Glenn put up a fight." Joan faked a smile, as if something on the television could have amused her. "The pajamas he wanted were in the laundry." She rose as Stanton crossed the room to the stairway, but she resisted the urge to take his arm.

"I'll kiss them goodnight." Stanton nodded slightly, evidently pleased with this idea. He looked at his boots and used the pine banister to pull himself onto the first step. Joan positioned herself by the rail to make sure he did not fall. When the toe of his boot caught on the carpet of the third step, Joan was there to grab him. Stanton was a small man, outweighing Joan by only ten pounds, and she had little trouble getting him back on balance. It was when Stanton could again hold onto the banister that he turned and glared at Joan, his jaws clenched, the muscles in his cheeks and temples bulging.

Joan pulled her arms against her sides, protecting her ribs. She looked upstairs, to Glenn's and Paula's rooms and hoped neither was awake. Stanton slapped her in the face, his hand slightly curved, the sound much like that of ground beef dropped onto a kitchen counter.

Joan's vision blurred instantly. Stanton knocked her from the bottom step nearly to the floor, but she used the halogen lamp to steady herself. Stanton licked his teeth. He didn't call Joan's name as she went for the front door. Joan worked the handle clumsily, seeing everything through a red haze.

The air on the front porch usually felt cool and fresh to Joan on these nights, like the first breath following an escape, but it was chilly even for October. Though the frigid air helped cool her eyes, she could not help shivering. The air chilled her cheek, which she could feel starting to numb and swell.

The neighborhood was quiet and dark. Joan wanted someone to be out there, someone she could run to and explain that Stanton had never hit her in the face before, but she didn't know if she could stand the questioning, the sympathetic frowns she'd get from the neighbors once they knew. It was the senselessness of everything that got to Joan the most. Her life with Stanton was good otherwise. He kept his job and kept his thoughts to himself most of the time. If something was bothering him, Joan had no idea what.

The living room light went off, and Joan could hear Stanton fumble his way around the coffee table on his way to the television. For a moment, she thought he was coming toward the front door, and she hurried off the porch and started towards Newton Park, where she usually went to walk in the cool air and give Stanton enough time to calm down and fall asleep. Sometimes he got into Glenn's miniature bed and slept there, the child using one of Stanton's arms as a pillow.

The park was a quarter-mile away, in the center of town: a circular enclosure of grass, a playground, elm trees, all bordered by a red brick sidewalk that split Newton Road. The neighborhood there was one of municipal buildings and stores, vacant this time of night. As Joan walked, she saw Stanton come home over and over again.

On the redwood bench, under the only lamp in the park, Joan let herself cry. When she finished, she thought of walking among the elms for a while. Going back home was always the hardest part of these nights, but there was nowhere else for her to go.

It was a while before Joan noticed Elise Fiske, who was standing on the stone chess table. Elise was waving her arms and hopping up and down, as though hailing a cab. She was a slightly older woman who baked strawberry rhubarb pies and tuna-and-bean casseroles for holiday potlucks and played the witch who threatened to turn children into toads for the VFW haunted house. As Elise clambered off the picnic table and walked around the swing set, Joan covered her cheek.

"I've seen you out here before," Elise said, walking gingerly on the damp grass. She was wearing brown slacks and a Morris the Cat T-shirt. "I saw you a couple months ago," she said, "when it was still warm. You had on your housecoat, the pink one, the one that's quilted." Elise Fiske was known for a sharp memory of clothes, hats especially. Morris the Cat stared coolly out from her shirt.

Joan kept her focus on Elise's feet, aware that her lashes were still moist, her eyes red. Elise was wearing women's sneakers. The hole in her left sneaker betrayed the red toe-line of her ankle sock.

"I like the park this time of night," Joan said. "The air feels good."

"Sometimes I come out here myself," Elise said. She spoke with an inquisitive lilt to her voice, as though she were conducting an interview. "But I don't see you out here all that much." She bounced in place impatiently. She seemed in a hurry. "I usually go to Frieda's on Friday nights and help her bake." She pointed towards the section of town where Frieda Briar lived.

Joan kept her head down, but Elise just kept talking.

"Sometimes I just sit in the backyard and listen to the birds," Elise said. "Squirrels sound nice, but they get into our tomatoes and I have to chase them away. Sometimes I sit on the seesaw when you're not here and Frieda's not baking. When I do see you, I usually just keep walking, and you don't notice me."

Joan wanted to leave, but she knew she hadn't spent enough time out of the house yet. It was when Joan saw Elise lose her balance and nearly fall that she herself realized the woman was drunk. At this thought, she felt her eyes turn moist again, and she put the heel of her palm to her nose. Elise was standing before her, and they were alone, but Joan did not think that Elise Fiske, wife of Deputy Bertram Fiske, would know anything about her situation. The Fiskes were always one of the first couples dancing at the New Years' Gala at the elementary-school gymnasium. They played bingo and won occasionally. Bertram drove the Miss Flemington float in the Christmas parade.

It was getting harder to keep from crying again. Joan wiped her nose on her sleeve harshly. Elise was still staring at her.

"I'm okay," Joan said. She stood slowly, keeping her injured cheek turned away. "I'll go home now."

"I was going to Frieda's," Elise repeated, pointing the way.

Joan shook her head.

Elise kept her arm poised, as if she couldn't bring it down again. Frieda Briar was a widow and ran her own bakery. Friday was baking day. Saturday morning, people crowded Frieda's bakery for fresh bread, cake and hand-dipped candy. Joan knew where Frieda Briar's house was, but had never been inside it.

"It's just over there," Elise said. "Frieda's making taffy tonight. They're always up late baking, and Frieda told me they were making taffy tonight."

Joan was about to make an excuse about having to get some sleep when Elise said, "Bertram only yells at me. He tells me to get the hell out of his house and never come back." Elise was tapping her toe hurriedly, her eyes wide from too much liquor.

Elise led the way, crossing streets without looking for traffic. As she plowed forward she said, "It's just a couple of blocks," as if she knew Joan was thinking of giving up and heading home. Elise kept her hand out as they passed a telephone pole.

"We're nearly there," she said, barely avoiding a fire hydrant.

The streaks Joan's tears had left on her cheeks felt like dry spirit-gum. She wondered if she could peel her sorrow right off her face.

Frieda's pink delivery van with THE LOVIN' OVEN stenciled onto the doors was parked in the driveway. The front door to the three-story house was wide open, and the light inside made a long rectangle on the porch ceiling. It was hot inside the house, hot enough to make Joan slightly dizzy. Elise's glasses fogged up, and she cleaned them with her T-shirt as she led Joan to the kitchen.

The kitchen, double the size of any one Joan had ever seen before, looked dim through the fog of flour. Three women were at work, supervising the industrial kneader, making rounds among the eight ovens, pulling out browned loaves of bread and sheets of Halloween cookies and replacing them with unbaked dough that sat ready beside the ovens. Frieda was the widest of the three women, her apron tied at the back instead of the front. The heat and the sight of this huge woman prancing around this large kitchen were overwhelming to Joan. She thought of leaving and going back to the park, but Elise took her by the wrist.

"Frieda," Elise called, and Frieda turned quickly and started toward her, her face sour and businesslike. She clapped her hands together briskly and left a trail of flour smoke in the air behind her. Joan backed away in fear and respect, and Frieda practically pinned Joan in the hallway with her hip as she pointed toward another part of the house.

"The taffy pots are in the den," she said. "Take a free one and have someone tell me when they're all through. After I flavor them you can cut and wrap."

Elise nodded in an almost military style and started for the den, releasing Joan's wrist. Joan moved to follow, but Frieda grabbed her by the arm and pulled her into the kitchen. Joan resisted at first. The heat in the kitchen was too stifling, the floured air hard to breathe, but Frieda's grip was strong and she pulled hard. She looked at Joan as if she were about to scold her for being trouble.

Frieda pulled Joan over by the sink, which was half-filled with beaters and wooden spoons caked with dried batters. Measuring cups littered the counter, and Frieda looked through them until one met her qualifications. She cracked an egg over it and flipped the yolk from shell-half to shell-half until all the white had fallen. Joan was mesmerized by the woman's speed. Frieda scraped some flour from the counter and ran a little warm water in the cup. She mixed it all with quick, perfect strokes.

Frieda pulled on Joan's chin until the bruised cheek was facing her. Joan tried to resist again, but it only made Frieda pull harder. As Frieda dabbed her fingers in the measuring cup, Joan felt passive and scrutinized, like a patient at a checkup.

Frieda murmured, "This'll hurt a little," just before she patted Joan's cheek with her dripping fingers and rubbed forcefully. Joan winced, but kept still until Frieda stopped and said, "That should help some. Go to the taffy, now." Joan left the kitchen gladly, already feeling a film of sweat forming on her forehead and upper lip.

She found Elise on the floor of the den behind a pot of raw taffy. Elise had both hands in the mixture and was squishing and pulling at it, her face concentrated and determined. The strips she pulled at were already smooth, and they gleamed dully in the light. There were other pots of taffy on the floor, and Joan sat in front of one. Already she could feel her cheek beginning to dry, and she wondered if the poultice was going to flake off by itself.

"Just work at it," Elise said, pulling another large ball of raw taffy from the pot and working it with her hands. "This is a really good batch. It comes together nicely."

Joan looked down into the raw taffy in front of her and was reluctant to touch it–a potful of chunky off-white liquid, which looked more like something used to make a man-eating blob in a horror movie.

Elise wove her fingers together, breaking the webs of taffy between them. She let her hands back down into the pot with a slap. "This stuff is going to turn out fine," she said. Her forehead glistened, and she drove her hands deep into the pot, her face tense and serious as she worked the taffy together.

Joan could hear the clanging of cookie sheets and baking pans and the hum of the kneader at work through the wall. Slowly, she reached into the pot with both hands. The raw taffy surrounded her forearms like thick liquid, but her hands could grasp handfuls of the stuff. She opened and closed her hands in the taffy for a while, feeling the candy between her fingers, before she grabbed two handfuls and pulled them slowly from the pot. A long string of taffy followed her hands, and she kneaded the raw mixture a little before letting it back down. She had forearm-length taffy gloves, and her skin was warm. She looked over at Elise and smiled, but Elise didn't look up from her work. Joan followed her example, amazed at how well this batch was coming together.

HOMECOMING

I have no intention of revealing myself to these two passing arm-over-arm in front of my house. From my porch, they look more like twins, actually, their baseball caps, their identical flannel vests and beards. But when one suddenly veers from the sidewalk and collapses on my lawn, pulling the other along by the neck, I go out to them. The conscious one looks worried, and I would too: left alone, my twin suddenly dead during Homecoming Weekend in Gainesville, Florida.

"Hey, we're real sorry, you know," he says to me. He's down on one knee, his twin's arm still around his neck, and he holds his wallet out to me as if in consolation. The wallet flips open in a professional manner.

This man's name is Ryan, and he is a Mountie. His ID picture is poorly lit, and there's "Canadian Mounted Police" stamped in a comic gold above the photo. Ryan doesn't have quite the accent I think Canadians should have, but still I don't doubt him.

"We were just looking for our ride," Ryan says, sounding American, really, like he's from up North, Pennsylvania perhaps. He struggles to get his twin's wallet out. "Me and my partner Temp here, we're real sorry."

The partner's name really is Temp. A Canadian name, I guess.

Temp's far gone. He was doing Kamikaze shots at The Monkey, a bar a few blocks away. All the bars around here are named after animals. Ryan was doing some too, but he knew his limit. Temp just kept slamming Kamikazes back, and now he's like this. This is what Ryan explains to me, and I realize he's talking to a guy whose lawn he just collapsed on. He doesn't know me at all, doesn't know what I might be able to do, even if I did want to do anything to either of these guys, and he's talking to me like we've known each other a while, a month at least.

Looking at him now, up close, I can see he's lanky compared to Temp, his face thinner.

I offer Ryan a Benson & Hedges, which he takes, saying, "Hey, wow, I could use a fag." Some sayings don't go out in Canada, I guess.

Ryan uses my lighter and takes a long drag from the Benson & Hedges. After exhaling, as if the smoke has given him strength, he shrugs off Temp's arm, and Temp falls flat to the grass.

"Yeah, we came down here to see a buddy of ours," Ryan explains, "and we came down for the game, but we lost him somewhere in The Mullet or The Porpoise." Ryan shakes his head and says, "We were just walking back to his house, but we don't know where it is."

I'm not surprised. This being a university town, there is a lot of cheap housing that look a lot alike. There's a Burger King nearby, a Gate Food Post, a Krispy Kreme Doughnuts, even a Hare Krishna house, but most of all it's two-, three-bedroom houses, indistinguishable from each other in the dark.

Not that I much belong here. I've been here only three months, myself. All I have to do with the university is the library, where I work, reshelving books the students leave about.

"He drank six pitchers, him and this other fella," Ryan continues. "He just wouldn't stop, and now look at him." Ryan can barely put his words together. "We don't know even who this guy was. We walk into The Monkey, and he tells us at the bar sit with him so he can buy us drinks. Everyone loves Temp."

I nod, but I'm jealous. They're not even from this country, and people buy them drinks. I don't get along with the university kids at all. I'm more than twice their age and don't know what being in a university is like. I'm from Alabama, a small town called Amsterdam, that has nothing like this: 4-Runners racing down the street, kids whooping and hanging out the windows, throwing beer cans. Kids pissing on the side of my house, right under my bedroom window. A white guy with a steel pole taking a swing at a black guy. "You want to fight?" The black guy yells out, "I'm going to kick your ass," and the white guy drops his pole and runs. (This happened in the street right in front of my house.) One block down from me is the Hare Krishna house. The Krishnas serve lunch on campus—curry, rice, and a sweet, yellow dish with wheat germ in it. They come by my porch after lunch, carrying empty pots and banging tambourines. When I'm there, they call out, "Hare," and I don't know what to say back.

One block the other way is a co-op. Eighty students all living together. I guess the building used to be white, but it looks gray now. They're proud of where they live, and they made a float for the Homecoming Parade: a wire and crepe-paper alligator, the university mascot, Al Gator, chomping on a South Carolina Cardinal.

All night, there's been a couple sitting on the float, drinking and pinching each other. Every now and then, the girl will squeal playfully.

The wildest Amsterdam, Alabama ever got was Mardi gras. Old Louisianiers would escape the wave of tourists and come to Alabama to go swimming, so we'd have a Mardi gras parade every year with one float. Miss Amsterdam, our grade-school beauty, rode in the back of a flatbed, the Amsterdam Elementary School Choir singing "Accentuate the Positive" and "Tiger Rag," Miss Amsterdam throwing Moon Pies. The black kids from the other side of town came in for the parade, and they beat each other over Moon Pies—they scratched and pulled each other's hair and screamed nasty words.

I drove the truck myself, sometimes. The only hard part was watching out for the black kids in the street. Aside from that, it was pretty much always a nice spot to be in. People were so excited about waving that they'd wave to me too, and I'd wave back. They'd ask me to honk my horn and I'd oblige. My wife and daughter would come out just to see me drive by. I'd blow them kisses. My wife would put our little girl on her shoulders, and they'd both wave. No matter how big our little girl was getting, my wife kept putting her up in the air like that, though after a while it was only my daughter who was waving anymore...

A blue Ford races by, KC lights blaring, the truckbed full of fraternity kids with beer cans. The kids hold their beers out to us.

"Go Gators!" they scream. They do train whistles and wolf howls, and they're past and gone before you know it. Ryan stands and almost falls, all the while yelling, "Yeah, go Gators!" but the effort is slow-going, and Ryan isn't even on his feet before the truck is gone. Still, Ryan yells, "Go Gators," again, as if the truck were just around the corner, hushed and listening for us. Ryan looks up to the sky and yells, "Go Gators," like it's a universal truth, the all-binding force of the universe and of all fellow men. His words even carry a hint of an echo.

Ryan then sits back on the grass, facing me, and says, "So, you're a sportsfan?"

I nod and I smile. I'm not, but I don't want to tell Ryan this.

"Yeah," Ryan says, "me too. Me and Temp here." He points, as if I don't know who he's talking about. "Me and Temp come down every year for this. Temp loves it," Ryan tells me. "They love him down here. People are always asking him to tell jokes, and he's great at it. Aren't you great at it?" Temp doesn't respond, and Ryan continues. "He tells all these jokes, and he sings, and these kids love it."

Ryan laughs, and I laugh with him. When we're both done laughing, there is an uncomfortable quiet. It's quieter than it's been all night. Even the kids who were sitting in front of the co-op are gone. I can hear Al Gator's crepe paper rustle in the breeze.

"So what do you study?" Ryan finally asks.

What can I tell him? Three months ago, my wife announced that our marriage was over? That I didn't believe her, but still I called her bluff? Can I tell him this: that I packed up a car, all the while thinking any moment she was going to stop me, and when she didn't, I left, believing with every ounce of hope I could muster that in a week she was going to want me back, and that the farther I drove, the sooner that call was going to come? Can I tell Ryan how long I drove, no music, hardly a stop except for the barest of necessities? Counting the breaks in the lane markers when I was tired of watching the odometer, then forgetting to count them, then wondering if I had passed a million yet? How can I say I only stopped in Gainesville because it was in my way and I felt I couldn't drive any longer?

Why does it seem almost impossible not to tell him?

"I don't," I come out with, cautiously. "I work at the library."

"Hm. I got to get Temp home," Ryan says, almost as if I haven't said anything at all. "We fly in the morning, and I don't know where our buddy is. He's got a white T-shirt. His name's Sammy. No one calls him Sam. He's got a T-shirt, says, 'I'm Standing And I Can't Fall Down!'" Ryan laughs, like he just got the joke.

Temp even chuckles.

It's the first sign of life I've seen from Temp, but he doesn't wake any. Ryan says, "Yeah, Temp," like he's happy to see this as well, and he looks at me and says, "Temp's a real card. You should've seen him dance on the bar. He danced on the bar. He almost took his pants down, and the kids in The Porpoise loved it and they booed when the bouncers threw us out. They sounded like they were going to tear the place up, they loved Temp so much."

I try picturing Temp on the bar at The Porpoise, doing a jig, undoing his belt. I can easily picture the university kids cheering him on. From what I've seen, it's not hard to please university kids, though they don't like me. They piss on my house and leave books for me to pick up everywhere, but they love this drunken Mountie who will take his pants down in a bar. My own wife won't even return my calls anymore.

Ryan and I give Temp a throne. Ryan helps me drag my vinyl recliner with the broken footrest from the porch, and we put it out on the lawn and get Temp into it. Temp has a belly on him, and he looks in his early forties, somewhere around my age, and he's so limp it's hard dragging him around. His head droops dangerously when we lift him by the arms. The recliner lever won't budge, but Temp looks comfortable just the same.

I run inside and get a wastebasket and blanket. The house is dark, and I fall over things, I'm in such a rush. I trip over the coffee table and then the phone cord, and I don't even bother to put the phone back in its cradle. I'm afraid that the Mounties will be gone if I take too long, recliner and all. Just gone.

"Hey, that's great," Ryan says, spotting me with the stuff. I spread the blanket over Temp and tuck him in. Maybe it's the grinning Blue Jay on his cap that makes me think he's smiling. Ryan puts the wastebasket next to the recliner, leans in and whispers in Temp's ear, "Hey, man, here's a bucket."

Still not opening his eyes, Temp turns and throws up in the wastebasket. Ryan pats Temp on the shoulder; these guys are close. They probably have dinner together, kiss each other's wives and make jokes about swapping.

I want Ryan to wake Temp up so he can tell me some of these jokes, sing me some songs, and if it's that easy, I think this is something I'd be able to do. I can sing.

Ryan looks concerned. "He's had an awful lot," he says, and this isn't a boast. Temp is finished, but he stays poised over the wastebasket, a thin line of drool hanging from his lip.

"But we're leaving tomorrow," Ryan says, disappointed. "We got a plane to catch, so we better get a cab." He moves to stand. "Can I use your phone to call a cab? I gotta call a cab."

I show Ryan into my house. The house could hold a family, a small one, if all the rooms were habitable, but they're not. The floor to the laundry room is so brittle that I break pieces from it when I'm thinking about things. There's a hole in there from a washing machine that fell through the floor. The washer's still there. It doesn't work and it's rusted, so I know this place has been falling apart for years. There are three bedrooms, and the ceiling is about to cave in on two of them. It's what makes this place cheap enough for me to afford, but when I look at the doors to those two bedrooms, all boarded up, the house feels painfully empty, and sometimes I'll do things like go out to one of the bars and call my wife's voicemail when I get home and apologize for everything I can think of, or sit all night on my porch and smoke Benson & Hedges until I get dizzy and fall asleep in the very seat Temp's now passed out in, so when I lead Ryan in, I feel good. I have company, though he's only coming in to call a cab so he can leave. Ryan has the number to the cab company memorized. The address of the house he's staying at is in his wallet. It's on the other side of town, a long way from here. Afterward, we go back outside.

"They said it would be twenty minutes," Ryan says once he's down the porch steps. I don't know if he's saying this to me or Temp.

Temp must have thrown up again—the blanket is ruffled. Fresh dribble on his chin. I have an urge to tuck him back in, make him comfortable so he, at least, won't want to leave, but I don't act on it.

"Tell me a joke," I say to Ryan. "Tell me one of Temp's jokes."

Ryan has gone out to the sidewalk. He's leaning out into the street, expecting the cab already. He's wobbly, and he looks ready to fall. "Nah," he says. "Only Temp can do them. There's one about a koala bear in a whorehouse, but I can't remember. Temp's the one with the jokes." He tries to get up on his toes, but can't and has to give up.

I turn to Temp. "Maybe you should get him up anyway, so he'll be ready to go when the cab's here." I can't believe I'm saying this, but I want to hear this joke. What would a koala bear do in a whorehouse? If it's funny, I'll be able to tell someone else. Maybe the brunette who works at Reference. She smiles at me. I could go to The Monkey and tell it to a waitress or a bartender. I could tell it to someone in line for a Krishna lunch. I know a few jokes, but they're not funny, and almost everyone knows them already. What do you call a woman with one leg shorter than the other? Eileen. That's the kind of joke I know.

Ryan doesn't pay much attention to me. He's looking both ways down the street, though it's one-way. He looks at his watch, adjusts his cap, and looks down the street again.

Time is moving. A minute has passed, at least.

Then something happens. It's a crash, the sound of the float being tipped and kicked. Ryan is staring down the street towards the co-op, and when I look that way myself I can see a Camaro parked in front of it. Four guys have tipped the Gator float and are kicking the wire and crepe-paper alligator all to hell.

"Those sons of bitches," Ryan yells. He's ready to bust heads. "They're busting Al! They're busting the goddamn Gator!" He cups his mouth at this last statement and yells it down the street, like he's sounding the alarm, and the guys from the Camaro seem to understand this—they run back to their car. Students are coming out of the co-op, running and shouting "Stop!" and "Hey!" but the Camaro pulls away, accelerating with a roar, and as it passes us, the kids inside stick their hands out the window and give us the bird. They call us faggots and dick-wads. Ryan is looking around for something to throw, and from behind us I hear:

"Fuck you, assholes."

It's Temp. He's raised an arm, the middle finger fully extended. The finger is short and fat, but noticeable all the same. "Fuck you, assholes," Temp says again, and Ryan goes to pieces. He falls down, he's laughing so hard.

"Yeah, Temp," Ryan says. "Yeah, Temp, you tell them, Temp. You show those mothers." Temp keeps his arm and finger raised, and Ryan looks as though he's about to kneel before Temp and praise him. I know how he feels.

The students from the co-op ask us from down the street who those guys were, and Ryan says he doesn't know. Just a bunch of drunk fucks, he guesses, probably a bunch of pissed-off Cardinal fans. The students start down the street towards us, about ten of them. Some of them have six-packs in their hands, and they're coming towards us.

"Fuck you, assholes," Temp says one more time, and he leaps from the recliner. He staggers across the lawn and onto the sidewalk. He points himself towards the students who are coming at us, and he starts a jig, a little Jackie Gleason number, his arms bent at right angles.

"Yeah, go," Ryan yells, and now I can see Temp doing this on top of a bar, his belt undone, his pants starting to fall. It's a wonderful sight, and I laugh myself.

But the jig doesn't last long. When Temp falls, he falls backwards a long time, because his feet keep moving, keeping him up. He doesn't want to fall, it's obvious, not now, but gravity's working on him. Then he can't keep his feet anymore, and he comes down onto the pavement, the back of his head hitting with a loud smack! the Toronto cap flying off his head. Temp is bald, very bald, and though the hit sounded painful, he's smiling, and Ryan is laughing, and the students are laughing, but I'm concerned as all hell. This is the second time tonight I think Temp is a dead man, but Ryan only kneels down next to Temp and picks his head up.

"That was a great number, partner," Ryan says.

I see headlights again, down the street. It could be the Camaro, but it could be the cab. I wonder if there's any way of getting the students to sit on my lawn and have a beer so Temp can tell them some jokes. Temp's eyes are shutting again. He's taken one hell of a hit, and he's losing consciousness. The students are practically here.

"Get him up," I tell Ryan.

Ryan looks up at me, confused. He's holding Temp's head

gingerly. "He's out, man," he says, and it's obvious that he doesn't even know my name.

"Get him the hell up," I say. "The cab is coming," I say, but that's not the reason. The students are practically here, and they're not going to stay without Temp. Everyone loves Temp. If I keep him on my front porch all the time, everyone in Gainesville will be calling on me. "Get his ass up," I say, and I reach down and grab Temp by the jacket.

"Whoa, he's hurt bad," Ryan says, but I don't want to hear it. The headlights are practically here, as well as the students. I'm not going to let Temp allow this opportunity to slip away. I pull on his jacket, and Ryan tries to undo my grip, but I won't let him. This is far too important to me.

THE CREMATORIUM

SWANTON - Adam Bernard Climie, 52, died suddenly Monday in his shop on Main Street. A Swanton resident for all his life, Mr. Climie was a plumber. Survived by wife, Ida, and son, Danny. Services will be held at the LaRe Home of Eternal Rest at noon Sunday. Potluck reception to follow at the home of Mr. Arthur Greenstock over the grocery store on Swanton Road.

—*Garrett County Gazette*, 10/21/15

Thin couldn't break a sweat—not from opening the oven hatch, the burners inside releasing flames high, bright and orange, not from loading the coffin from the rusted gurney onto the rollers alone. A good sweat, Thin thought, would be something healthy, something normal. Two weeks since the last cremation, and Thin had forgotten how hot the oven could get, but still he could not sweat. Adam Bernard Climie, inside the dark-oak coffin, didn't shift or flop at all: a well-packed casket. LaRe was the best mortician in Garrett County. After making sure the coffin was in place, Thin pulled the release lever, and Adam Climie rolled into the oven, bumping against the back wall and making the grill rattle. Thin sealed the hatch, muffling the sizzle of the oak's varnish. As he forced the bolt into place, Sammy came back in, zipping his fly. Thin took off his work gloves and checked his forehead for the slightest bit of hope, but still nothing. He put the gloves on the rollers and watched the glow of flames from the small, round window in the bottom corner of the oven hatch.

"Should have a barbecue," he said. "Me and Mary don't take the tots anywhere anymore." He made a list in his head: burgers, chips, Mary's macaroni salad with artichoke hearts, steaks, Genessee Cream Ale.

"How's she feeling?" Sammy said. He patted his pockets, looking concerned as he did so.

"You know," Thin said, still watching the oven window. He tried wiping his hands onto his overalls, but they were still black and stained. "Don't think this'll take too long?" He turned and looked at Sammy. Sammy was sweating like a hog. Thin added pork chops to his list, and applesauce.

"Pump up the flame." Sammy patted the outside of his pockets again and looked around the room. "That fat'll sizzle off quick enough. You seen the Luckies?"

"Huh?"

"Luckies. Lucky Strikes."

"What do they look like?"

Sammy walked around the room, bending to look under things. "You know," he said. "Luckies." He found a bottle wrapped in a brown paper bag under one of the chairs by the door. "Get over here," he said, "you sucker," as he swatted at it.

"This is a find." Sammy straightened up and blew something that resembled dust from the bag. He pulled out a half-pint of Grandad's, the label halfway free.

"Grandad's been down here a spell." Sammy wrapped the bottle with the bag again. He looked around the room some more and found a pack of Luckies on top of the switch-box.

Thin studied his hand. He couldn't understand. It looked normal to him, except for the scar, what Doc Goldberg called a disfigurement: damage to the peripheral ends of nerves in the epidermis. The first stage. A mild form of leprosy, Doc called it: nothing dramatic, but an infection just the same.

Sammy tapped a Lucky Strike from the pack and held it between his teeth. He held the pack in Thin's face. "You want?"

"Want?" Thin glared at Sammy, but Sammy continued to offer. Sammy's hand was stained even worse than his own because Sammy wouldn't wear gloves. Sammy was the only person outside of Thin's family who knew about the leprosy, but when Thin first told him, Sammy acted like it was all a practical joke. "When'd you start?" Thin asked.

"A while ago. You seen me." Sammy lit his cigarette with a lighter from his back pocket and took smoke into his mouth. "You want?" he said as he put the lighter back.

Thin looked at his own hand again and imagined disfigurements up his forearm, on his face, his legs. "Shit," he said.

Sammy put the pack in the pocket of his gray shirt. He worked the paper bag down the neck of the Grandad's. He broke the seal and drank.

"What do you do?" Thin asked. He imagined disfigurements on his chest and upper thigh, on his head, behind his ears. He imagined Mary's disgust at each and every sight of him, not to mention the tots, until they sent him away.

"Huh?" Sammy said. He puffed again, then drank.

"If your own wife doesn't want you around the tots? Your own tots?"

Sammy took another drag of the Lucky, another pull of Grandad's. He chuckled. "That bit again." He grinned and shook his head.

"Sammy." Thin narrowed his eyes into the most serious face he could make.

Sammy shrugged as though willing to play along. "It's all over then," he offered, and he pulled back another drink.

Thin looked Sammy over. Sammy was fat and had high blood pressure. It was his excuse not to load customers onto the rollers. "What if you just want parting words with your kids before you go?" Thin asked. "I mean, just so they have something to remember you by?"

"Face it," Sammy said. "It's all over." He started toward the door. "Maybe there's more meat," he said, though the plumber was the only cremation on the schedule for that night.

Thin looked at the disfigurement on his hand again. Doc Goldberg told him it wasn't fatal, and Thin knew this from looking up leprosy, but he also found pictures of severe cases, people who didn't have faces anymore, only bloated folds of flesh that looked brittle and dry, people who spent their lives in hospitals, living on and on. Doc tried to assure Thin that his case would never come to that, but who knew? Even Doc thought hospitalization was a good idea, just to keep everyone safe. One man allowed only his lower leg to be photographed, something Thin was thankful for after seeing that calf.

"Wait," he said, stopping Sammy in the doorway. "Better leave the bottle. LaRe might decide to do some snooping tonight," Thin lied, though he figured Sammy would know better. Still, Sammy left the half-pint on the switch-box. Thin took it and took a drink as he wandered back to the window on the oven hatch.

Adam Bernard Climie was burning well. Thin took another pull from the Grandad's and leaned against the oven. When he was first hired, fifteen years ago, he wore a rag over his nose and mouth because of the stench that came from the oven. Sammy called him 'Masked Marvel' then, but after a few months Thin didn't need the rag anymore. He wished he had gone to Climie's funeral instead of scrubbing out the oven. He wished he had taken a peek at the plumber before roasting him.

The hatch was getting too warm to lean against. At full blast, it was hot enough in there to melt a construction helmet in five seconds, hotter than Venus. Before Thin, there was a guy named Al who Sammy talked about on occasion. LaRe fired Al for flicking ashes on a customer. He smoked cigars, the biggest ones he could find, and once while hammering bone fragments to dust for the urn, he flicked, and LaRe just so happened to be looking in.

Thin drank and turned up the heat. The plumber wasn't going to keep him late. He decided to ask Sammy sometime whatever came of Al.

Sammy came in, handling his groin. "Know what I heard?" he said. "I heard this was big business during the Black Plague. And no one wanted the ashes. Customers just piled up in the oven."

"Nah." Thin leaned against the rollers. He felt tired. "Most just rotted in the street, from what I hear."

"A plague could keep us busy," Sammy said. "You tell LaRe we should get paid on condition."

Thin shook his head.

"You know," Sammy said, taking the Grandad's back, "by the customer."

Thin nodded.

"Yeah," Sammy said, "that way, we'd earn enough to get our own oven someday."

Thin liked this idea. "That way, we could do each other for free." He wanted to laugh and grab Sammy by the shoulders and ask him more about it, this idea, but Sammy didn't look excited. Sammy turned away, spat in the corner, and wiped his mouth.

"No thanks," he said. He drank, then said, "I'd rather explode."

Thin was about to ask, but Sammy had already put out his hand in explanation.

"Explode," he said. "Get a few cases of dynamite from Jerry, maybe some Roman candles, surround myself so I don't go flying one way or the other, and it'd just blow me to bits. Put on quite a show."

Thin wanted to turn the heat off and see what burning was like—just undo the bolt, pull open the hatch and see what was the first to go after the clothes, skin and hair, then slide the plumber back in and later take another look to see if the heart really went last, or if some of the larger bones, the femur or the cranium, held out the longest—but he knew Sammy would complain about the yellowish smoke a burning body emitted, so he turned the gas the other way, higher, making the window glow more fiercely.

"Easy, easy," Sammy said. He pulled out his Luckies.

"Do you have to?" Thin asked.

Sammy took a Lucky Strike and lit it. He puffed and blew.

The smell of Sammy's smoke was like the smell of the sparrow his oldest, Raymond, burned with lighter fluid in the back garden. The kid came running into the house, carrying the sparrow in a Cool Whip container. He yelled, "Daddy, Daddy, I did it," and he put the container in Thin's lap. Mary slapped the kid and chased him to his room while Thin could only stare, the bird still breathing sporadically, the black, burnt features broken by a thin trail of clear liquid coming from one of the burnt-out eyes. Thin took the container to the bathroom and dropped the bird into the toilet. There was a hiss when the sparrow connected with the water, and one of its feet crumbled off. Thin flushed and watched the foot, curled into a clutch, float, then spiral away. The water was dark with ashes, ashes everywhere. He looked at his hand again.

"Hey," Sammy said, "I just remembered a good one." He chuckled. "Heard it from a couple of orderlies back when I got that operation." He puffed and blew.

Thin wanted to turn the heat up as far as it could go and blast that plumber into ashes so he could get home. But he would have to sneak in if he wanted to hug the baby, as Mary locked the kids away when Thin came home. Besides, LaRe had told him on his first day of work, "If the flames get too high, the ashes scatter and you have to brush them out of every nook and crack."

"A leper walks into a restaurant and sits at a table, and this guy at another table keeps staring at him, so the leper goes, 'If I bother you, I'll leave.' The guy goes, 'Oh, no problem at all,' so the leper gets a meal, and the guy suddenly throws up all over his plate..."

Thin took the bottle so Sammy could use both his hands to tell the joke. He didn't know there could be so many leper jokes in the world. But the more he resisted them, the longer Sammy took to tell them. He drank, sat on the rollers, and tried to look bored.

"So the leper goes, 'Oh, I'm offending you, I'll leave,' and the guy goes, get this..." Sammy grabbed Thin's shoulder. "'It's not you. It's the guy behind you, dipping his bread into the back of your neck!'"

Sammy laughed hard. Thin chuckled a bit, though he didn't want to. He put his hand in the pocket of his coveralls and dug deep until he found the pamphlet about the special hospital. "I'm not really prepared to treat this," Doc had apologized. "I mean, you just don't expect this kind of thing to crop up in *Maryland*." When Thin was a kid, he had no idea who lived in that rundown house at the edge of town or why his friends dared him to sneak in there, steal something and come back out. All he knew at ten was that he was afraid of being called a chicken and spineless and a girl. The place was dark and thick with a rotting smell, a smell older Thin figured was the same one Mary complained about before she moved into the guest room. Young Thin could barely see, and he practically sat on the living room couch next to a wrinkled man, who had been asleep under a hand-knit flowered quilt. The leper grabbed Thin's wrist, his bare arm covered with disfigurements.

"Fucking kids," the leper growled. "Fucking obnoxious kids." A million to one shot, even larger, that an infection could be spread this way, but it had.

Sammy took the bottle back, still laughing.

"Hear any other good ones?" Thin asked. He hoped Sammy had a Polack joke or a black joke. Maybe a dead-baby joke, where dead babies got caught in blenders and on pitchforks and in Volkswagens: the good ones.

Sammy finished the half-pint and put the empty bottle on the floor, almost falling over, but Thin grabbed Sammy's arm and didn't let him. Sammy wiped his mouth on his sleeve. "Well," he said, "there's the one Father Schultz told me the other day: how do you get a nun pregnant?"

Thin took some time to think.

"You fuck her," Sammy said.

They both laughed a long time. Whenever Thin tried to stop, he would look at Sammy and keep going. He was feeling good until his stomach started to hurt, but he couldn't stop. It was Sammy who finally stopped first. He coughed hard, bending forward. He held his stomach and knocked the empty bottle over with his foot.

"Had to stop before I threw up." Sammy sighed and chuckled twice, but then made his serious face. "Check on our little chicken in there," he said.

Thin looked in the oven window. He couldn't see anything through the black paint on the glass except a glow from the flames.

"Nah," he said, and considered the flames some more. "But he's close." He started to laugh again, but rested his head against the oven door and stopped.

"Let's take a walk," Sammy said. "LaRe should be home eating dinner by now." He went out, up the stairs, past the storage room. Thin followed Sammy and didn't notice any change in the air at first. He sat by the door and rubbed his arms. Sammy stretched and belched. He groaned. He stretched again and walked around.

Thin wanted to bring up the barbecue, or Sammy's scar from his appendectomy, or that exploding idea—anything to get himself talking—but he kept rubbing his arms. He liked the feel in his hands, and he knew he would miss this. He leaned back against the cinderblock wall, closed his eyes, and concentrated on feeling his fingertips against his skin through his sleeves.

The next thing he knew, Sammy was shaking his shoulder.

"Should be done by now," Sammy said. "I'll fetch the can. You powder the bones."

"It's an urn," Thin said. "It's called an urn." Let the deceased have some dignity.

"Urn. Can. Thig-a-mah-jig. Whatcha-ma-who's-it." He was practically inside again.

Thin got up and stopped Sammy just inside the doorway. Sammy stared back at him. He had a smudge on his face.

Neither of them could ever leave the crematorium clean, no matter how careful they were.

"Got a Lucky Strike?" Thin asked. What was the point of denying himself anything anymore?

"Sure." Sammy reached into his pocket. He held the pack in Thin's face.

Thin took a Lucky, but when Sammy offered him flame, Thin couldn't bring himself to lean in towards it. It would have been easier to run back in, open the hatch and climb in with the plumber.

Sammy shrugged. He withdrew the lighter and went in.

Thin stayed outside at first and listened to a car drive by in the distance, probably going along Flowers Road. He looked down the hill at Swanton. He couldn't imagine how he lived there. He looked around the graveyard that surrounded him and couldn't picture a tombstone for himself that Mary would visit every Sunday with the children. Would Raymond remember the bird he'd burned and who he'd burned it for? Thin knew he was going to stop by Sammy's for beer before going home. They were going to watch some television, play some checkers and make plans to go out for beers sometime, plans that were never going to happen. He was going to miss this routine. He considered staying downstairs, by the oven. He thought about turning down the heat so that Mr. Climie could burn slowly. All night, maybe.

Thin went back inside. As he passed the storage room, he saw Sammy tap the end of his cigarette into the urn.

ABOUT THE AUTHOR

Richard Weems is also the author of the Amazon bestselling Cheap Stories eBook series, *Stark Raving Blue*, and *From Now On, You're Back*. He is a retired teacher living in upstate New York

More at www.weemsnet.net.

WHEN THE MIND SOARS

Poems from the Heart

MOMOH SEKOU DUDU

Forte Publishing

First Published in 2016
Published by:
FORTE Publications
#12 Ashmun Street
Snapper Hill
Monrovia, Liberia

FORTE Publishing
7202 Tavenner Lane
208 Alexandria
VA, 22306

FORTE Press
76 Sarasit Road
Ban Pong, 70110
Ratchaburi, Thailand

http://fortepublishing.wix.com/fppp

Printed in the United States of America

ISBN: 099453471X
ISBN-13: 978-0994534712